THE INT
DAM
Book 1

By the same author

THE INTIMATE MEMOIR OF DAME JENNY EVERLEIGH
BOOK ONE

THE INTIMATE MEMOIR OF DAME JENNY EVERLEIGH
BOOK TWO

THE INTIMATE MEMOIR OF DAME JENNY EVERLEIGH
BOOK THREE

THE INTIMATE MEMOIR OF DAME JENNY EVERLEIGH
BOOK FOUR

THE INTIMATE MEMOIR OF DAME JENNY EVERLEIGH
BOOK FIVE

THE INTIMATE MEMOIR OF DAME JENNY EVERLEIGH
BOOK SIX

THE INTIMATE MEMOIR OF DAME JENNY EVERLEIGH
BOOK SEVEN

THE INTIMATE MEMOIR OF DAME JENNY EVERLEIGH
BOOK EIGHT

THE INTIMATE MEMOIR OF DAME JENNY EVERLEIGH
BOOK NINE

THE INTIMATE MEMOIR OF DAME JENNY EVERLEIGH
BOOK TEN

THE INTIMATE MEMOIR OF DAME JENNY EVERLEIGH
BOOK ELEVEN

The Intimate Memoir of Dame Jenny Everleigh

Book 12:
Forbidden Escapades

WARNER BOOKS

A *Warner* Book

First published in Great Britain
by Warner Books in 1993

Copyright © 1993 by Potiphar Productions

The moral right of the author has been asserted.

A CIP catalogue record for this book
is available from the British Library.

ISBN 0 7515 0143 3

Photoset in North Wales by
Derek Doyle & Associates, Mold, Clwyd
Printed in England by Clays Ltd, St Ives plc

Warner Books
A Division of
Little, Brown and Company (UK) Limited
165 Great Dover Street
London SE1 4YA

This is for David and Sir Louis

Introduction

This explicit, uncensored account details the secret life of an upper-class Edwardian young lady and if nothing else, this novel shows how quickly the strait-laced Victorian dam of iron-clad respectability was breached in the early years of the twentieth century by a powerful current of sexuality which had been building underneath the repressive public morality of the previous decades.

In fact, this surge had burgeoned earlier during the latter decades of Victorian Britain, perhaps as a reaction against the stifling social *mores* of the time – and this reaction was fuelled by the lusty lifestyle of no less a personage than the Prince of Wales himself, a man of robust and varied sexual proclivities, whose many affairs were known to many outside his 'Marlborough House' set of close friends.

Furthermore, as Dr Louis Lombert drily commented in *His Mighty Engine*, the seminal study of underground magazines of this period: 'Our picture of the age is one of smug, aggressive puritanism, of demure, downcast eyes, of chaste maidenly blushes and stern-faced, bewhiskered gentlemen standing solemnly before ornate mantelpieces in richly over-furnished drawing rooms. Yet surely in the great population explosion of the late nineteenth century, there must have been some sensual enjoyment (however socially illicit), some revelling in the so-called Sins of the Flesh, some private beliefs indeed that sexuality was not sinful at all.'

Without doubt, a far more relaxed attitude prevailed after the ascension of Edward VII to the throne and in general terms we associate the Edwardian era with a freer, more modern outlook regarding social affairs. During the first years of the century, a reforming Liberal government introduced old-age pensions and national insurance, laying the foundations for the welfare state and, in the teeth of fierce opposition from Tory backwoodsmen, Lloyd-George curbed the excessive privileges enjoyed by the unelected and unrepresentative House of Lords.

Of course King Edward VII himself contributed much to the whiff of sexual scandals which pervaded the air of London in the 1900s and it is no real surprise to find that his name often features in the Jenny Everleigh stories for they merely confirm Edward's inventive approach to sexual delights. The jolly King makes an appearance in *Forbidden Escapades*, a lively, erotic tale and this leads me to believe that it may well have been at least partially penned by Estelle Kenton-Waller, whose torrid liaison with Edward in the late 1890s (when he was Prince of Wales) so horrified Sir Lionel Trippett, one of the Prince's senior equerries, that he wrote to his sister that: ' . . . all we hear from HRH day in and day out is of the beauty of his lovely Estelle . . . the woman is devilishly attractive but I fear that she has cast a spell upon him and I am fearful that some great indiscretion may occur. For he is simply besotted by Lady Kenton-Waller and spends every spare moment of the day with her. And as for the hours of darkness, the less said the better.'

Sir Lionel had genuine cause for concern but fortunately for all concerned, the passionate affair cooled down and the *mari complaisant*, Sir Michael Kenton-Waller was rewarded for his silence by the post of deputy Lord Lieutenant in the county of Yorkshire (not Middlesex as erroneously stated by my old friend Professor Roger Yougger in his otherwise excellent informative introduction to *Jenny Everleigh 7: The Honourable Member*, a position which took the Kenton-Wallers far from the wild goings-on amongst the Prince's London circle.

Therefore I would speculate that the graphic royal sexual shenanigans described with such relish in *Forbidden Escapades* were probably based upon the illicit weekend enjoyed by Edward and Estelle at Woodway House, the Sussex country seat of the wealthy Kirkrup family during April 1898, and may have indeed been written by the lady herself who, under the pseudonym of Prudence Radlett, published three books of children's stories just before the outbreak of World War One.

However, it is more likely that Estelle recounted all the juicy details to Belinda, the

3

daughter of Sir Marmaduke and Lady Gertrude Kirkrup, for this fiery girl was one of the trio of radical young feminists who actually wrote the *Jenny Everleigh* diaries, using intimate experiences culled from their own or from their friends' love lives as their source material. The diaries were first printed in the *Oyster* and other *sub rosa* erotic underground magazines and have been unavailable to the general public until they were successfully republished some one hundred years later.

By all accounts, Belinda Kirkrup was the most fiery of the three girls (the others being Geraldine Newman and Heather O'Fluffert) who dreamed up the diaries to shock the Establishment by challenging widely held tenets such as young people (and girls especially) should be kept ignorant about the facts of life. As the social historian Godfrey Elton-Stanton wrote in his foreword to *Jenny Everleigh 4: The Secret Diaries*: ' . . . women were believed to have no sexual passions, though if they felt twinges of desire it was their bounden duty to suppress them! But the Jenny Everleigh diaries are proof of the rebellion against a notion which appears so ludicrous a century or so after its propagation.'

Now we can all smile at the classic anecdote of the Victorian mother's advice to her daughter on what she should do on her wedding night – 'lie back and think of England' – but to many girls, without prior knowledge of their own bodies let alone of any male appendages, this was all the instruction they were ever given. As Mr Elton-Stanton says: 'It was their lot to put up with stoicism with men during their "baser moments" and for an unmarried girl, it was constantly drummed into her that one act of sexual intercourse would lead to her "ruin" . . . these unyielding axioms caused much distress to both men and women alike and as such were ridiculed by the popular underground magazines. Here the joys of sexuality were uncompromisingly asserted and perhaps these publications owed their popularity not only because of their unashamed efforts to arouse but also because they created an acceptable place for sexual behaviour in the minds of their readers and assured them that sex offered enormous pleasures for both male and female alike.'

The uninhibited erotic vitality of the Jenny Everleigh tales spans surprisingly freshly across the years. One sexual adventure presses hard on the heels of another but the sheer energy and variety never flag thanks to the high-spirited wit and imagination of Belinda Kirkrup and her cohorts. Furthermore, the amusing vignettes of upper-class Edwardian life are made more pungent by the lively bawdiness which made the books so immensely popular amongst the *cognoscenti* of the time. The chronicling of sexual adventures served a useful purpose, being published in an atmosphere when so many were racked by guilt, and even more were in blind ignorance about their bodily functions.

Like all the graphic Jenny Everleigh stories, this lusty narrative eschews the darker deviancies of her age such as under-age sex and sado-masochistic flagellation, though a liberal, open-minded tolerance runs through the entire salacious, splendidly entertaining narrative.

Charles Whetstone
BOURNEMOUTH
JUNE 1993

'I saw you take his kiss! ''Tis true,'
'O, modesty!' 'Twas strictly kept:
He thought me asleep; at least, I knew
He thought I thought he thought I slept.'

Coventry Kersey Dighton
[1823–1896]

Chapter 1

May 21st, 1909

'Cast ne'er a clout, till May be out,' I said thoughtfully whilst the wind howled and great globulets of rain spattered angrily against my bedroom window as a sudden summer shower burst through the grey, leaden skies.

'Too late, my dear Jenny, we've already casted,' grinned Geoffrey Manning as he sat up and threw back the bedclothes, exposing our nudity to the sparrow which had perched on the window-ledge.

I pulled back the eiderdown over us and I returned his smile to which the young rascal replied, 'Oh, come on, Jenny, please don't cover yourself up. You know how I adore feasting my eyes on your delicious naked body.'

What a smooth-tongued scamp was this new young man in my life, diary, truly a man who could charm the birds off the trees and I dare say it was his witty yet erudite conversation as much as his handsome face and broad, well-built body which led me first to offer luncheon and then, to Geoffrey's great delight, the opportunity to sample the joys of *l'art de faire l'amour* with me.

However, as with any good story, it is best to start at the beginning – Geoffrey and I had met the previous week at a picnic down in Sussex which had been organised by my dear, lovable chum, Miss Kathie McGonagall. Those who have perused my account of a previous journey I made in this lovely part of the country [*see* Jenny Everleigh 8: Business As Usual – *Editor*] will recall that Kathie and I became bosom pals (in every sense of the phrase!) after our first meeting on a sunny August afternoon in Dr Jonathan Claydon's bookshop situated in the tiny village of Falmer on the Lewes–Brighton road.

For readers unacquainted with this episode I should perhaps mention that at the precise time I entered the premises, Kathie was being fucked doggie-style by her employer in the stockroom whilst I waited patiently in the shop with Messrs Barry Gray and Bob Warner, two senior representatives of the distinguished publishing company of Jackson and O'Connor, who had arranged an appointment with Jonathan Claydon to show the dirty doctor the most saleable tomes from their firm's list of forthcoming titles for the Autumn and to solicit orders from him for these interesting new volumes.

The same evening, after Kathie and I had enjoyed a tribadic exploration of each other's bodies whilst Bob, Barry and Jonathan carried on their literary discussions in the Dog and Duck, we all travelled to Brighton for a splendid if lascivious party at the Hotel Splendide during which we both sampled to the full the many delights afforded by the sturdy pricks of our three stalwart gentlemen.

Since those erotic revels Dr Claydon had decamped to San Francisco but before leaving he left Kathie a generous farewell present of one thousand guineas which she has used to open her own bookshop in Chichester which she runs with the aid of Marcella Pyecombe, a pretty young girl who has just returned to England from Madame Helene Dupont's Finishing School for Young Ladies on the banks of Lake Lucerne in Switzerland.

Anyway, I was delighted to receive a letter from Kathie inviting me to come down to Chichester and spend a weekend with her, especially as I had recently decided to finally break off my relationship with Sir Edward Hammersmith. Although he was a fiery lover and we had much in common besides the enjoyment of many blissful nights of passion, I could not for a moment entertain his proposal of marriage, even though I was flattered and pleased to have the lusty baronet go down on his knees to beg for my hand. 'I cannot imagine why you should want my hand, Edward,' I told him rather unkindly. 'You've already had my pussey, titties and bum.'

The truth of the matter, diary, is of course that I am not yet ready to settle down into the matrimonial state. I firmly believe that unless there are justifiable causes – as for instance with poor Lady Paula Plattslane [*see* Jenny Everleigh 10: Canadian Capers – *Editor*] whose husband soon made known to her his homosexualist preferences of the kind which led to the downfall

11

of poor Oscar Wilde and refused to perform his conjugal duties more than three times a year – married couples should stay faithful. I am a firm believer in the institution of matrimony and have never knowingly entertained a married man with the sole exception of His Royal Highness King Edward VII, God Bless Him!

Quite frankly, at present I am enjoying myself far too much to change my ways – no doubt I will someday meet a gentleman with whom I wish to spend the rest of my life, but for now I am determined to keep playing the field.

However, I must return to the very start of my marvellous weekend holiday with Katie and Marcella which led to my first meeting with Geoffrey Manning, for it all turned out to be quite an adventure which richly deserves to be recorded for posterity.

May 17th, 1909

The fun began only an hour or so after I had left our new London house in Belgrave Square, early on the Friday morning, and bid farewell to Mrs Caughey, our trusted old housekeeper who was the repository of many of my intimate secrets. Papa and Mama had been out of town for three days as they were spending a week up at Sandringham at one of Queen Alexandra's informal little gatherings and as they had travelled to Norfolk in Lord and Lady Dyott's motor car, I decided to let Osbourne, our chauffeur, drive me to Chichester in Papa's new

Rolls-Royce rather than go down by train.

We had just passed through Guildford and were cruising at a steady thirty-five miles an hour when a loud bang from the rear of the car woke me from my light doze and I was treated to the sight of Osbourne straining to keep the vehicle on an even course.

'Nothing more than a puncture, I hope?' I enquired whilst Osbourne steered the car to a halt on the side of the road and pulled up the handbrake.

'I shouldn't think so, Miss Jenny,' replied Osbourne, getting out to inspect the damage. I opened my door and followed him to the back of the car where we gazed at the pavement-side wheel which was already resting on a flat bed of rubber.

'I'm dreadfully sorry, Miss, I must have driven over a big nail for the blinking tyre to go down so quickly,' said Osbourne gloomily.

I tried to cheer him up and said, 'Never mind, Osbourne, you can't be blamed and anyhow, we're carrying a spare, aren't we?'

The chauffeur's face coloured up to a bright shade of beetroot red and he mumbled, 'Yes, Miss Jenny, of course we are, but I'm afraid that we don't have any of the tools I need to change the wheel.'

'No tools? Why on earth not?' I stormed at the unfortunate fellow. 'Did a burglar break into our garage and steal them?'

He hung his head and muttered, 'No, Miss, we've not had any burglars. What's happened is that just before your parents left London, the master gave me instructions to polish up everything in the toolbox and I've clean forgot to put it back.

'I'm awfully sorry, Miss,' he added miserably. 'I meant to put the box back of course but I very foolishly allowed myself to be distracted just before we left. It suddenly struck me that I'd left it behind in the garage after about five minutes but I didn't think it was worth mentioning and worrying you unnecessarily.'

'You should have done, Osbourne,' I said sternly. 'It was almost inevitable on a long journey that we might have to make some repairs, even with such a superb machine as a Rolls-Royce.'

There was a long silence as I gazed out angrily on to the open fields – the sun was now shining brightly and paradoxically the beautiful warm weather seemed to cool my anger. In any case, my philosophy has always been that we all make mistakes and, if at all possible, genuine expressions of contrite apology should always be accepted. Certainly Osbourne deserved credit for his courage in admitting to his error as opposed to trying to pin the blame on somebody else which, I was aware, he could quite easily have done.

I took a deep breath and said, 'Well, there is absolutely no point crying over spilt milk. Where exactly are we?'

'About two and a half miles from Godalming, I would reckon, Miss Jenny.'

'A small town might not boast a garage,' I mused as I fumbled for some coins in my handbag, 'but there'll be enough opportunity to hire a horse and cart there as well as the services of two or three strong young men who will be glad to assist you for, say, five shillings each. Here's some money, with luck you might cadge a lift but if not, the walk will be your penance for being so forgetful.'

My chauffeur took the money and said shamefacedly, 'Thank you, Miss Jenny, I'll be as quick as I can.'

'Well, off you go then,' I said briskly but he stood stock-still for a moment, twisting his cap around in his hands and it suddenly occurred to me that he might think that he was under pain of instant dismissal either in Chichester or when we returned to London. So I added, 'You don't have to fret, Osbourne, I'm not planning to mention this incident to my parents.'

I waved him away with a tiny smile and he trotted off towards Godalming whilst I took out the rug from the motor and carried it into the pleasant shrubland at the side of the road. I laid it down on a level stretch of earth beside a tree and then returned to the car for a magazine, a cushion and a bottle of ginger pop and soon I was sitting comfortably in the warm sunshine, licking my lips as I read the latest scandals in the columns of *Cremorne*, a magazine which I dare not purchase myself, but happily my cousin Molly Farquhar kindly sends me her copy through the post every month after she has finished with it. [This spectacularly rude underground magazine was published quarterly by the Society of Cremornites, a London-based epicurean dining club whose semi-secret wild parties were occasionally attended by the Prince of Wales in the late 1890s – *Editor*]

There was a charming letter in the magazine from a Miss Merida Hatfield which caught my eye. Although only nineteen years of age, Miss Hatfield (daughter of the Reverend Cecil Hatfield, the Rector of Upper Loxford in Warwickshire) was an expert typewriter [the appellation of 'typist' to a girl who could use one of these new-fangled machines was not in general use until the 1920s – *Editor*] who had gained the position of personal secretary to Sir Felton Renshaw, the well-known art historian and critic.

I found Miss Hatfield's letter so interesting, diary, that I shall reproduce all but the introductory paragraphs in your pages. The dear girl began by stating how one afternoon she had been working in the study of Sir Felton's palatial country house, correcting a manuscript written by Sir Felton on the sixteenth century painter Sofonisba Anguissola, a little-known Italian female artist of the sixteenth century, when there was a knock on the door . . .

'Come in,' I cried and rather sheepishly Sir Felton's sixteen-year-old son Radleigh came into the room, carrying one of the large leather-bound volumes of prints which his father kept on the top shelves of his extensive library.

'Yes, Radleigh, what can I do for you?' I enquired but the lad shook his head and said politely, 'Nothing thank you, Miss Hatfield, I've only come in to return this book which I borrowed yesterday morning.'

Now I was glad to see that young Radleigh was at last taking an interest in his father's work because, much to his parents' concern, he appeared to show little interest in the arts – or indeed any academic subjects according to his school reports. However, the slim, good-looking youth had broken several school athletics records and had recently been appointed captain of football. Nevertheless, Sir Felton had confided his worries to me and I was pleasantly surprised to discover that Radleigh had been leafing through one of his father's books.

So I rose from my desk and said to Radleigh, 'What pictures have you been studying? Some works of the old masters or have the modern impressionists charmed you?'

I stretched out my hand, thinking that he might show me the book he was clutching in both hands but strangely the boy brushed passed me in an attempt to climb quickly up the stepladder that was leaning up against the wall behind me and replace the tome before I could see what it contained. Unfortunately for Radleigh, this stratagem failed when he caught his foot on the bottom rung of the stepladder, causing him to stumble and lose his grip on the book which slid out of his grasp and on to the carpet by my feet.

Naturally my curiosity had now been aroused and I picked up the book and opened it up. Well, I suppose I should have guessed what kind of art young Radleigh had been so keen to study! Yes, he had been gloating over a set of coloured photographic plates which his Papa had purchased from the executors of the estate of the late Sir Lionel Trapes, the former Permanent Secretary at the Treasury who was perhaps the most famous collector of gallant literature in all Europe.

I picked up the book and as I slowly flicked through two or three pages I thought to myself that Radleigh had certainly chosen one of the most erotic sets from the

17

notorious Trapes' collection. The photographs had been taken by the Continental master Adrian Klein using a double quarter plate camera able to capture the full tonal range of delicate skin and the colourist was none other than Countess Marussa of Samarkand who lived with Monsieur Klein in Paris for several years.

No wonder Radleigh had been embarrassed to show me these photographs. They showed a beautiful young couple coyly named Abelard and Eloise who were seen first in the first picture lying naked together side by side in bed. He was a fine, strapping, broad-chested fellow of perhaps twenty-two or twenty-three years of age with long, fair hair and light brown eyes whilst the girl (who could not have been above twenty at most) was most attractive with flowing dark locks, a seductive full mouth and a coltish figure with small but pert breasts, a smooth, flat belly at the base of which sprouted a luxuriant dark bush of curly hair that set off her long legs and through which one could just discern the outline of her pussey lips.

In the next pose, Eloise is pictured on her knees with Abelard's massive erect cock in her hands with her open mouth teasingly near his uncapped knob and on the following plate the camera captures her performing sweet suction upon this lucky youth's stiff shaft. Her tongue is shown washing the sensitive underside of his helmet whilst her lips are open wide, ready to take this succulent sweetmeat inside her mouth. Then her pretty head is seen in close up, her eyes closed in ecstasy as she sucks his immense tool with at least half the veiny shaft between her lips and her hands caressing his heavy ballsack.

I turned over several pages to see the inevitable conclusion which turned out to be a doggie-style

18

coupling with Eloise on her knees with her rounded bum cheeks stuck high in the air and Abelard with his meaty prick jammed in the crevice between her bum cheeks. From a careful study of the angles I judged he was fucking Eloise's cunney as opposed to attacking her rear dimple and this was confirmed in the next photograph where Abelard was shown flat on his back with the delicious girl still impaled on his glistening cock which one could see was firmly embedded in the juicy haven which nature intended.

The lucky girl, I thought to myself, it's been a full three months since I have had the pleasure of a sturdy thick prick reaming out my juicy love channel. My breasts tingled and I could feel a moistness between my thighs as I hastily shut the book only to see Radleigh standing beside me, the material of his tight grey trousers stretched to bursting point by the bulge in the front.

The only excuse I can make for what followed is that my blood was up, fired by Monsieur Klein's superb photographs, for I reached out and gently stroked the throbbing swell. 'Well, we've both seen the game, haven't we, Radleigh? The question is, would you like to play it with me?'

'Oh, I'd love to, more than anything else in the world!' he gasped, his face flushed with such excitement that the delightful thought suddenly occured to me that this fine young man might still be in virgo intacto.

'Now you must tell me the truth, Radleigh. Am I right in thinking that you have never played before?' I said softly as I deftly unbuttoned his flies.

He bit his lip and muttered, 'Yes, but I promise you, Miss Hatfield, that I'm more than ready.' I must have looked a mite doubtful because he added quickly, 'and if you don't believe me, ask Daisy, the blonde chambermaid, and she'll tell you!'

'Tut, tut! I believe you, dear, but I thought you just said that you had never –.'

Radleigh cut me short and went on hurriedly, 'I've never gone the whole way, Miss Hatfield,' and it was my turn now to interrupt.

'Merida, please, call me Merida,' I murmured, fishing inside his trousers for his prick which I brought out to see for myself. It was of surprising thickness for one so young and I feasted my eyes on the hot velvet-skinned pole which bucked and bounded in my hand.

'So you've yet to travel the full distance, my lad,' I smiled, releasing his stiffie to unbutton my blouse. 'Well, I dare say it's time you did. Tell me how Daisy comes into the reckoning whilst we take off our clothes.'

'Take off our clothes?' he queried, his voice rising in an almost fearful anticipation.

'Of course, dear, fucking in the nude is always far preferable,' I said coolly as I walked to the door. 'Don't worry, I'll lock up here whilst you unlace your shoes.'

When I had done so I kicked off my own shoes and said gaily, 'Now tell me about you and Daisy.'

'There's not much to tell,' he said shyly as he unbuckled his belt. 'It all started one morning a few days before my sixteenth birthday last February. I had just taken a bath and was standing in front of the mirror whilst I was drying myself. But as I rubbed the towel around my groin, my chopper began to swell up and well, I wasn't in any great hurry so I dropped the towel and began to play with my prick. Then in the mirror I saw Daisy behind me standing in the doorway. I picked up the towel to cover myself but she just laughed and

20

closed the door behind her.

' "Oh Master Radleigh, you're very well developed for your age! A big boy like you deserves a treat," she said and she pulled the towel away and cupped her hands around my quivering cock. She began to slick her hands up and down my prick and she whispered, "Do you like that, Master Radleigh?"

'I should say I did! But all I could do was to nod my head because I was too excited to reply. She tossed me off very quickly and since then we've had a kiss and a cuddle though there haven't been many opportunities as I'm only here during the school hols. Daisy's let me squeeze her titties whilst she wanked me off but we've never gone further than that.'

By now we had both undressed and I could see Radleigh devouring my curvy naked body with his eyes. I took him by the hand and led him to a big black leather couch. Then I gave his cock a friendly squeeze as I arranged the cushions before laying myself carefully down on the sofa. Even at this late stage I felt a qualm about taking the handsome lad's cherry but there was little doubt that he desperately wanted to lose it and besides I had taken him down the beach to the edge of the sea and it would be wickedly cruel to deny him the chance to bathe.

I held his body as he lowered himself upon me and when he settled himself I reached down and guided his youthful cock inside the slippery gates of my love lips and I gasped as his shaft slid inside me, filling my cunney which was now becoming very wet indeed. I spread my legs well apart to enable him to push down to the hilt and poor Radleigh trembled all over, visibly overcome with the emotion of his first actual experience in fucking.

He lay motionless and I looked up at him in surprise and said, 'Is something wrong, Radleigh? Doesn't it make you feel good to have your cock in my cunt?'

'Merida, it's marvellous! My God, I've been dreaming of this moment for years!' he cried, his voice fairly cracking with fervour as with something like a sob he then confessed, 'but frankly I'm not very sure about what I'm supposed to do next!'

I tried hard not to giggle and just about managed to succeed and I said gravely, 'It's all very easy, dear, just push in your lovely cock as far as it will go and then pull it out except for your knob. Then push forward again and repeat the exercise in a brisk rhythm.'

To encourage him I slipped my hands round each cheek of his boyish backside and pulled him towards me, feeling an odd thrill of achievement at the thought of being his first woman – and I can attest to the fact that what the boy lacked in experience he made up for in enthusiasm, bouncing up and down on me as I clutched at his jerking bottom, wrapping my legs about him and heaving myself upwards, doing my level best to pull him further into me as I panted, 'Go on, Radleigh, fuck me hard! I'm going to spend any time now! Shoot your spunk inside me, you young scallywag!'

Being Radleigh's first fuck, I knew that he would spunk sooner rather than later so I called upon my much admired ability to contract my pussey muscles around his shaft which was now sliding in and out of my honeypot at a great rate of knots, and I shuddered in anticipation of a delicious spend as his balls tightened and he poured a copious libation of hot, sticky cream inside me.

To my delight, Radleigh did not have to rest before continuing this joust, being a young man at the peak of

22

his powers. He only had to rub his glistening wet tool for a few moments and it swelled up again to its full height. I lay back and he plunged his prick inside my twitching cunney, this time riding me with more confidence and I had to cling on for dear life as I lifted my bottom, rotating my hips wildly to achieve the maximum contact.

Radleigh groaned and I felt his body stiffen and his fingernails digging into my back as his shaft suddenly popped out of me and slid crazily across my tummy spurting frothy white spunk all over my skin. I do believe that the lusty lad would have managed a third cockstand but we were interrupted by a knock on the door from Bristow the butler who announced that afternoon tea was now being served in the drawing room.

So we swiftly dressed and made ourselves as tidy as possible before going downstairs and taking tea with Radleigh's Mama, Lady Renshaw, and his uncle, General 'Black Jack' Chelmsford of the Household Cavalry. Unfortunately there have been all too few opportunities for me to continue Radleigh's sexual education but you may be assured, Mr Editor, that he has been a most diligent pupil.

I have the honour to be, Sir, your most obedient servant,

Merida Hatfield

I leaned back against the trunk of the tree whose leaves had protected me against the fierce rays of the midday sun. I closed my eyes and smoothed my hand down the front of my dress, pausing between my legs where my pussey had begun to moisten soon after I had started to read Merida Hatfield's licentious letter.

I stood up and looked around carefully to make sure no one was watching. Then I raised my skirt and pulled down my knickers. I stepped out of them and lay back against the tree-trunk as I slid my skirt up to my waist and slowly slid my hand up to the top of my thighs. The tip of my forefinger dallied for a few moments around the edges of my blonde pubic bush and then I closed my eyes as with the other hand I fondled my breasts whilst my finger slid into the wetness of my passion pit; as I parted the lips of my pouting pussey I purred with pleasure; as I stroked the soft folds of skin I thought how exciting it would be to feel the wild, throbbing tool of a strapping lusty lad like Radleigh between my legs.

My hands became busier, forming little circles now over my aroused clitty, pressing, cajoling, tickling until I felt the first stirrings of a forthcoming spend. My left thumb slipped inside my slit and I frigged myself off to a pleasant but hardly memorable climax – I would have far preferred to have my hands raking Radleigh's back as his raging young cock slewed in and out of my eager, dripping crack.

This reverie was broken by the sound of an approaching horse and cart. Hastily I dropped my skirt and, scrambling to my feet, I walked briskly back to the roadway and peered up the hill towards Godalming. It was surely too soon for

Osbourne to return yet I hoped against hope that this cart would be carrying my chauffeur and the helping hands he needed to change our wheel.

And yes! As the cart drew nearer I made out Osbourne's rather portly figure next to the driver and I could also see that there was another fellow sitting in the cart behind them. I waited impatiently for them to arrive and when they drew closer I could see that the driver was a good-looking young chap around my own age dressed in a short-sleeved white shirt and white flannels.

The cart pulled up and Osbourne hastily climbed down and said, 'Miss Jenny, there was an inn just about a mile away and I met this gentleman there who kindly offered his assistance.'

'Hello there, Miss Everleigh,' called out the driver and from his impeccable speech I knew straightaway that he had to be the scion of an upper-class country family. 'Your man here has told me of your plight and I would be delighted to help you if I can.

'However, may I first introduce myself? Johnny Lockwood at your service, Miss Everleigh and that young scamp in the cart is Harry, my young brother who has kindly consented to play cricket for our side this afternoon even though it's a far cry from the Eton v. Harrow match at Lord's.'

So that was why he was dressed in white – I smiled at Mr Lockwood and said, 'A pleasure to make your acquaintance, sir. It is most kind of you to come to my aid and I do hope that I won't have made you late for your match this afternoon.

After all, my cousin Philip Wingate is a keen cricketer and I know how important it is to attend the team talk before the start of play.'

'Gosh, is Phil Wingate your cousin, Miss Everleigh? My goodness, what a small world! Why, we played together for the Old Carthusians team only last Saturday up in Suffolk.'

I looked closely at Mr Lockwood and said to him, 'Now is that why I am not totally surprised that you know my name? Did we meet at some cricket match? I do very occasionally watch Philip play when I visit my aunt and uncle at their home in Dorset. Your face is definitely familiar to me, Mr Lockwood, though I must confess I just cannot quite pin-point exactly where we have met before.'

'Oh, Miss Everleigh, I am honoured that you should even recall my face,' he said as he jumped down from the cart, 'after all, we met only briefly at Lord Morgale's Charity Ball For The East End Milk Fund at the Savoy last November. Before the dinner, we were introduced by a mutual friend, Sir Gerald Newman, at the tombola stall.'

'Of course! How remiss of me, Mr Lockwood, not to have recognised you immediately,' I said especially as I now remembered admiring Mr Lockwood's physique at the time. He was a handsome fellow with thick, curly hair. He had neither moustache, beard nor whiskers which gave him a youthful if not boyish appearance. His eyes were warm and kind and I was much taken with his easy, friendly manner.

Young Harry Lockwood now jumped down from the cart with a bag of tools and Johnny (for we were soon on first-name terms) made the necessary introductions. Harry was proportioned on very much the same lines only at seventeen and a half was a trifle more slimly built, though he was tall for his age and if anything was slightly taller than his older brother.

It took less than fifteen minutes for the tyre to be changed but Johnny Lockwood insisted that I take luncheon with him. 'What about your game?' I protested but he laughed and said, 'That presents no problem, Jenny; the match is between a West Surrey Gentlemen's eleven and The Charlatans, a scratch side made up of members of the Reform and Jim Jam Clubs.'

'The Jim Jam Club,' I echoed with a smile. 'I wouldn't have thought many members of *that* establishment were interested in any outdoor sports!'

[The Jim Jam Club in Great Windmill Street was a fashionable meeting place for the ultra-fast set from the late 1880s till the Club was disbanded soon after the beginning of the First World War in 1914. In previous Everleigh novels, Jenny describes some of the free and easy goings-on there such as the monthly Victor Pudendum contest which was much favoured in the 1890s by the then Prince of Wales – *Editor*]

'No, I don't suppose there are,' he replied with a merry twinkle in his eye. 'But on the other hand I belong to the Jim Jam and so do Lord Herbert Whitechurch, Allan Burton and Geoffrey Manning who are turning out for us this afternoon.

'Do join us, Jenny, we're going to have a picnic as the weather's so jolly,' he continued as we stood by the cart. 'Your man here can have a good feed in the servants' hall and you can continue your journey whenever you please. I promise that you won't be forced to stay and watch the cricket!'

Well, I had always planned to stop somewhere for luncheon as Kathie McGonagall was not expecting me much before four o'clock so I gratefully accepted Johnny's kind invitation.

Johnny turned out to be a perfect host in the absence of his parents who coincidentally were spending the summer months in Italy with other relations of mine, Uncle Anthony and Aunt Phyllis Farquhar whose daughter 'Madcap' Molly's sexual exploits have filled many pages in this diary. Anyway, it was now so warm that I unburdened myself of my motoring clothes and slipped on a thin white cotton dress through which (and I must admit I knew this full well) the generous contours of my breasts and bottom would be seen in the great shafts of golden sunlight.

I unpinned my hair and let it cascade down my shoulders as I let Johnny Lockwood escort me down to the field where the picnic for some half dozen members of the West Surrey eleven was to take place. 'The other chaps are coming down after luncheon,' explained Johnny and he introduced me to the rest of the party.

Now I had expected a simple meal but picnics at Lockwood Hall were very grand affairs complete with roast chicken, roast beef, salads of every description, apple dumplings, a compote of pears, biscuits and pastries all washed down with some excellent wines and mineral waters.

'Good heavens, how on earth will you be able to

play cricket after such a huge luncheon?' I asked as a servant brought round cups of hot coffee.

'Very easily, Miss Everleigh,' replied a broad-shouldered young man with a mop of curly, dark hair whose name was Geoffrey Manning. 'We always bat first and our openers never partake of our pre-match feast!'

This answer made me chuckle and enquire as to what happened if they lost the toss and the opposing team decided to bat. 'Oh that problem never occurs, Miss Everleigh,' said Geoffrey, producing a coin from his trousers which he handed to me. 'You see, we don't lose the toss very often.'

I looked at the florin which at first seemed unremarkable – until I turned it over and saw that the King's face adorned both sides! 'A double-headed florin,' I remarked. 'It must be extremely rare.'

'Extremely rare and extremely valuable,' remarked Johnny Lockwood as he wagged a reproving finger at Geoffrey Manning. 'May I have it back, please, Jenny? Strictly speaking, tampering with the currency is a criminal offence so I'd be grateful if you kept mum about our little ploy.'

I promised not to reveal their secret and Geoffrey Manning said, 'Did I hear that you're bound for Chichester this afternoon, Miss Everleigh? What a coincidence, I'm going there myself for the weekend after the game. May I ask with whom you are staying?'

'Yes, of course you may though I doubt if her name will mean anything to you for she does not mix in Society,' I replied as we strolled down to the field of play. 'I will be a guest of Miss Kathie McGonagall of The Priory in Polesden Grove.'

'For heaven's sake, so will I!' Geoffrey cried, slapping his thigh. 'By Jove, how super. Tell me, did you come across Kathie when she worked at Jonathan Claydon's bookshop in Falmer? You did? Ah, then you might not know that she only helped out Jonathan because her parents cut her allowance when she refused to marry some suitable but boring young man her Mama had picked out for her. Kathie's main interest is in English folksong, a hobby she shares with my sister who is secretary of the London Folksong Society, which is how I came to know her.

'Well, I will look forward to seeing you again later tonight,' he added and tipping his hat to me, walked off to join his friends in the large tent which the teams used for a pavilion.

I sat down on a bench and waited for the game to begin. There were only a few scattered groups of spectators, mostly of workers from the Lockwood estate for Johnny had given as many staff as possible the day off. It was hardly a surprise to see the opposing team take the field after what Geoffrey Manning had shown me but it was Johnny Lockwood who came up to stand by my bench and he said, 'Can't you stay for a little while longer, Jenny? I'd love to show you round the grounds.'

'That would be very nice but isn't your presence required elsewhere?' I queried but he shook his head. 'Not really, bowling's my *forte* and I bat at number nine so unless there is a major collapse – which is doubtful as their best spinner

30

has been called up unexpectedly to turn out for his county second eleven – I won't be needed for the best part of two hours at least.'

'In that case I accept, kind sir,' I said as I rose from my seat. We walked about half a mile through some woodland through which ran footpaths and shady walks until we found ourselves in a sheltered, hidden cove.

'Shall we sit down for a while?' he suggested and pointed to a hummock of dry earth which had been covered over by a large woollen rug.

My eyes opened wide and I said with a touch of irony, 'Now isn't that amazing, Johnny, I never knew that rugs grew so well in this part of Surrey.'

He had the grace to blush as we sank to the ground. 'Actually, we haven't had too good a crop this year, there hasn't been enough sunshine though our legs will stay in the sun even though our bodies will be in the shade,' he replied as he slipped his arm round my waist.

I put my finger to his lips and we sat in silence for a minute or so whilst I enjoyed the sensation of being in Johnny's embrace. I leaned back against a pile of branches and opened my legs slightly and I was torn between irritation and giggling when I realised that I had left my knickers in the field I had been sitting in whilst I waited for Osbourne and the Lockwood brothers to make the necessary repairs to my car. I was cross because I had inadvertently thrown away a perfectly good article of clothing but I was amused to see the look on Johnny's face when he realised that in the glistening light he could make

31

out the outline of the silky curls of my pussey through the thin material of my dress.

Without further ado Johnny kissed me beautifully, nibbling my ears as he whispered his desire to make love to me whilst his calm, obviously experienced fingers caressed and massaged my breasts, opening the buttons of my dress and plunging his hand inside to roll my nipples into erection whilst my pussey became decidedly damp, moistening like a dew-drenched flower in eager anticipation of what was to come her way.

Our mouths met and our tongues fluttered together as we pressed even closer. Then Johnny broke off from the embrace and murmured, 'Dear Jenny, your pussey looks divine. Lie back and let me pay homage to it for I am certain that you will taste sweeter than any of the cream cakes we ate at the picnic.'

As if by magic he produced a pillow from behind him which had been hidden under a bed of leaves. Tenderly he placed my head upon it and lay down on the rug between my legs. I made no resistance as Johnny parted my thighs and lifted up my skirt to totally expose my honey blonde bush to his delighted gaze and I must state here and now that the dear boy proved himself to be an exception to the general rule that Englishmen (as opposed to the French, Italian and Scots) are poor pussey eaters! To my great delight Johnny Lockwood turned out to be an expert in this neglected art and I began to spend from the moment I felt the tip of his tongue gently parting my pussey lips, swiftly darting inside my cunney as I moaned softly with the pleasure this afforded me.

He placed his lips over my clitty and sucked it into his mouth with one hand now under my bum to provide extra elevation and the other round my thigh to enable him to spread my pussey lips with his thumb and middle finger. He soon found the magic button under the fold at the base of my clitty and he wickedly twirled his tongue all around it. The faster he vibrated his tongue the more excited I became and I gyrated madly as he moved slowly along the silken grooves of my cunt, licking and lapping my tangy juices which were now flowing as fast as a mountain stream. With each delicious stroke I arched my body in ecstasy, pressing the erect clitty against the tip of his flickering tongue.

'Aaaah! Aaaah! A-a-h-r-e!' I shrieked, yelping with joy as my climax sent waves of exquisite pleasure coursing through every fibre of my frame and whilst I lay gasping with joy, Johnny pulled off his clothes which gave me sight of his stiff, erect penis.

I reached up and took hold of his sturdy shaft which throbbed like hot velvet under my touch as I kissed the uncapped mushroom of his helmet. Then Johnny asked if he could have the pleasure of taking me from behind and as I have never had the slightest objection to being fucked in this way, I readily consented to his wish. This will not surprise you, diary, for you know that it has always been a source of surprise to me that any girl would listen to those misguided moralists who frown upon doggie-style copulation. Personally, I find it most stimulating because fucking doggie-style enables my partner to play with my breasts and my pussey and as Doctor Nigel Andrews comments in his wonderful book *Fucking For Beginners*, this position was widely practised by the ancient Egyptians and is currently extremely popular amongst the Eskimos and the Chinese as well as being perhaps the most favoured technique of fucking in Latin America.

So I kissed his cock a second time and raised myself up on my knees and turned away from him, provocatively wiggling my ripe, rounded buttocks as I said, 'Go on, Johnny, see how much of that thick prick you can cram inside me – but be careful, I don't want you to go up my bum.'

'I won't,' Johnny promised as he leaned over me and I soon gloried in the feel of the crown of his cock nudge against my yielding cunny lips. He pushed on and slipped his throbbing tool inside me, gently moving backwards and forwards in slow rhythmic thrusts as my juices eased his passage as he pushed in, withdrew, pushed in, withdrew, as I shivered with voluptuous ardour for I have yet to discover any feeling of pleasure that even approaches the delight of that first initial penetration of my juicy cunney by a big fat meaty prick.

Johnny's penis thrilled my stretched love channel for he used his cock like a master craftsman, varying the angle and speed of the joust and his staying power was immense. We must have been fucking for at least ten minutes before he concluded the performance when with a hoarse bellow he drenched my cunt with frothy wads of creamy jism and I echoed his cry as I too achieved a glorious spend.

His cock stayed hard in my honeypot for a little longer and then he slowly withdrew, his shaft glistening with our mingled juices and, though I am sure we were both game for another fuck, alas *tempus fugit* and it was time for Johnny to return to the pavilion and for me to find Osbourne and continue my journey to Chichester.

Johnny begged me to return to Lockwood Hall on the way back from my weekend. 'Do come and stay for a few days, Jenny, we would have a jolly time together, I promise you,' he said, squeezing my hand and I was very tempted to accept there and then.

'I'd love to say "yes", Johnny, but I think I had better find out just what Kathie McGonagall has planned before making a commitment,' I replied as we waved to his brother Harry who was shouting at us from the distance.

'As soon as I know more I'll send you a telegram,' I added as Harry came running towards us.

'There you are, Johnny, come quickly, you'll be needed to bat any minute now,' he called out.

'What on earth are you talking about? I go in at number nine!' said the astonished captain of the West Surrey Gentlemen.

'If you don't get a move on you'll be going in at number ten,' said his young brother grimly. 'I'm afraid we've collapsed against the attack of the two fast bowlers in the Charlatans team, and we've only twenty-nine on the board with seven wickets down. I went in at number four and knocked up twelve runs but that's by far the highest score so far though Geoffrey Manning's scored seven and he was still at the crease five minutes ago when I left the pavilion to look for you.'

A frown creased Johnny's handsome face as he drew a deep breath and said briskly, 'Right, well, I'd best run on and pad up in case I'm needed quickly. Harry, will you escort Miss Everleigh back to the ground.'

'Oh dear, I'm afraid that it's my fault that your team has had to play without the benefit of your captain's presence. Johnny might have been able to suggest some tactics and steady the nerves if he had been there.'

The slim lad shook his head and said, 'No, I don't think he could have helped very much, Miss Everleigh. These two Charlatan chaps are county players and I'm afraid we're out of our class, though I don't think we've done too badly considering that the pitch was watered yesterday. Still, they'll find that we'll have a surprise for them when we take the field as we've also got a guest player in our team, Mr Alan Brooke, the England and Middlesex leg spinner, and their batsmen won't find it easy to knock up a decent score especially with a wicket-keeper like Mr Manning behind them ready to pounce if they stray outside their territory. He stumped five batsmen earlier this season in our game against the Old Aberdonians.'

'Really? I had no idea that Mr Manning was such a distinguished sportsman,' I commented as we walked briskly towards the field of play where I noticed that Johnny had now taken his place at the wicket although it was Geoffrey Manning who was facing the bowler.

I clapped my hands in glee as Geoffrey dispatched the next ball to the boundary for four runs and I said to Harry, 'I see what you mean about Mr Manning, he does have a splendid eye for the ball.'

'Oh yes, and he plays hockey for the Southern Counties and soccer for the Corinthians during the winter. I think he is one of the finest sportsmen in England,' added Harry who obviously hero-worshipped the gentleman who would be joining me later at Kathie McGonagall's weekend get-together. [The Corinthians were composed of public school and University players whose code of conduct was so sporting that if the teams were awarded a penalty which was in any way disputed by the opposition, the kicker was instructed by the captain to shoot wide of the goal – *Editor*]

We were standing by the side of the pavilion when I turned to Harry and was startled to see the boy's face blush crimson and I happened to gaze down and noticed a prominent swelling between his legs. Surely he could not have seen his brother fucking me! What could have made his youthful cock swell up so? Rather than having a cockstand, his thoughts should have been fully occupied with the game, I said to myself, joining in the applause as Geoffrey hooked the ball down to long off for another two runs.

Then it struck me that the strong sunlight must be shining through my dress and Harry could make out the outline of my breasts and bottom, a sight which had so excited his brother. He saw my look of concern and blushed an even deeper shade of red. I had no wish to embarrass the poor boy but the thought flashed through my mind that I might well be in a position such as described so eloquently by Merida Hatfield in the *Cremorne*.

Funnily enough, if Harry were a novice in *L'art de faire l'amour*, it would not be the first time I had plucked a cherry during a cricket match as those who have read the columns of my earliest diaries will know [*see* Jenny Everleigh 4: The Secret Diaries; incidentally these entries were purposely dated 1871 instead of 1891 to save the blushes of some of the participants in one of the frankest Everleigh books in the series – *Editor*].

I simply could not prevent myself enjoying a little chuckle as I said, 'Dear me, I must apologise to you, Harry, for I see only too well how I've taken your mind off the game.'

He gasped and attempted to cover up the offending bulge in his trousers with his hands as he blurted out, 'Oh goodness, I'm, um, oh gosh, I'm deucedly sorry, er –'

I took instant pity on the poor love and said to him soothingly, 'Now, now, Harry, it's perfectly natural for a young man to find his prick jumping to attention at the merest fleeting glance of a scantily clad girl. Why, I am sure that you have already found out that occasionally your cock will erect itself for absolutely no apparent reason. Am I right?'

Harry gave a small lop-sided grin and nodded his head and I continued, 'Tell me, have you ever had the opportunity to use your equipment other than using your own hands to play with it?'

He looked so soulfully at me with his large brown eyes that I had a fancy to ravish him on the spot and then in a hot whisper he informed me that he was yet to cross the Rubicon into manhood.

'Well, you have nothing to be ashamed of, my dear,' I declared as I slid my arm round his waist. 'Why, stuck in your boys-only school what chance have you to find some female companionship?'

'It's really terribly kind of you to say so, Miss Everleigh –'

'Do call me Jenny,' I interrupted.

Harry gave me the most beautiful fresh-faced smile and began again, 'It's really terribly kind of you to say so, Miss Ev– Jenny, but I know there's at least one chap in my class named Bell who has found a couple of willing girls in Harrow village and they even like going to bed together with him.'

'Indeed? Are you sure? If you don't mind my saying so, exaggerated boasting is not uncommon amongst schoolboys.'

'Oh no, it's true all right – I happened to hear the two girls in question talking about him in the post office and they were saying how Eddie – well, as they put it, how Eddie can keep his prick as stiff as a board even after poking each of them in turn.'

I made a mental note to remember the name of Master Edward Bell who obviously possessed a physical prowess which would stand him in good shape when he left Harrow School and entered Society.

However, I digress – I took Harry's hand and pulled him to the ground behind a nearby clump of bushes. Then I took my dress and chemise together in both hands and lifted them up over my head so that I now stood naked before him, my nipples proudly standing out as I stroked my breasts. I lay down beside him and took his unresisting hand and placed his fingers around my left breast.

'There, how does that feel, Harry?' I muttered lewdly as I let my own finger stray down to the straining protuberance between his thighs. 'Do you like my titties? Why don't you suck them for me, there's a good boy.'

He needed little urging to obey and his mouth came down almost instantly to meet the rubbery strawberries as his hands gently pushed my bosoms together and his tongue came forward to circle my already erect little nipples. Then his lips opened and drew in the two red bullets, his tongue constantly moving which sent a series of marvellous vibrations shooting down my spine. Then I guided his hand down towards my blonde thatch of pussey hair and he let his fingers run through the silky pubic muff.

My cunney fairly throbbed with desire as my juices began to drip from me in a warm, sticky wetness. Harry's mouth was now glued to my titties, his lips sliding over each nipple in turn as he inserted first one, then two and finally three fingers in my juicy honeypot, pressing in and then releasing them in such an assured manner that I started to wonder whether in fact he had fibbed to me about being a virgin. But when I questioned him afterwards he confessed that Miss Thompson, the assistant housekeeper at Lockwood Hall, had in fact shown him how to handle a lady and indeed had once or twice rubbed his prick up to boiling point though she had never let him spend for fear of marking their clothes.

'How unfair of her,' I exclaimed as my body writhed under the lovely stimulation afforded by his finger-fucking my sopping pussey. 'Did you not ask her to carry on what she had started?'

He shook his head and I said, 'Ah, well you must learn not to be so shy. Always respect the wishes of your partner and do remember that if she says "no" then she means it and only a cad will try to force her to do anything against her will. On the other hand, as the poet says *Quae dant, quaeque negant, gaudent tamen esse rogatae*, whether they give or refuse, women always appreciate being asked!'

But this was no time to teach sexual manners to this lusty youth – now my back arched with ecstasy as his skilful fingertips slithered over my aroused clitty which sent me into a delirium of pure joy and if the combined teams of West Surrey Gentlemen and The Charlatans had gathered to watch I would not have been able to prevent myself from leaning over and tearing open Harry's trousers to release his pulsing prick. I was far from disappointed when I saw his bare cock for it must have been at least seven inches long and was of a fine thickness. His shaft was slightly curved but as smooth as satin to the touch. Unlike his brother, Harry had been circumcised and as I have been regularly fucked since the age of nineteen by dear Sir Ronnie Dunn who adheres to the Mosaic faith, naturally I am no stranger to such cocks. Like most liberated ladies, I have no inherent preference one way or another but I do prefer clean ones and my sensual appetite has been quickly turned off by a man who does not keep the underside of his foreskin free from unpleasant-smelling smegma.

I shook a fringe of hair away from my face as I lowered my lips to take his glowing round knob inside my mouth. 'What a delicious-looking prick,' I whispered to bolster his confidence. 'I feel truly honoured to be the very first girl ever to suck it.'

I opened my mouth and sucked slowly, working my way round the tiny 'eye' on top of the bulbous dome, catching a sticky drop of jism which had already formed there. I ran my lips all around the knob before opening my mouth and gulping in his pulsating pole. 'Ooooh!' Harry panted and in a single movement he forced some three inches of hot cock and I had to make him retract slightly until it lay pulsing motionless on my tongue. Then I closed my lips over this monstrous priapic lollipop and moved my tongue across its width, sucking salaciously on his lovely thick tool and I twisted my body round so that Harry could lean across to kiss my pussey and complete what would be a most agreeable *soixante neuf* if the youngster could eat pussey as admirably as his older brother.

To my great joy, Harry had read *Fucking For Beginners* and now put into practice the valuable lessons he had learned from Doctor Andrews' book, a copy of which should, in my opinion, be given to all sixteen-year-old boys and girls.

My body shook with delight, as without hesitation Harry buried his face in my groin and started to circle his tongue around my dripping slit. I felt his mouth flick across the grooves of my cunney which set off fresh spasms of delight crackling through me. However, I could not wait to be brought off by his tongue so I gently took his head in my hands and said softly, 'Now Harry, this is the moment you've been waiting for – I want you to fuck me,' and as I spoke there was a further burst of applause as Geoffrey Manning hit a further boundary. 'Take your time, dear boy, there's no hurry.'

I grasped hold of his yearning cock and I spread my legs wide open before guiding his fat helmet to my pink pussey lips which were swollen with desire. With a heartfelt sigh, he pushed forward and heavens, his magnificent prick pounded into me with the excited power and speed one would expect during a first time fuck. Despite my plea for him not to rush the proceedings poor Harry spent very quickly, shooting a fierce stream of spunk inside my tingling cunt. But the young scamp's shaft stayed stiff even after he had spent and with a deep groan he thrust his cock straight back again and began fucking me again without the slightest problem. His hairy ballsack slapped against the backs of my thighs as I wrapped my legs around his lithe body and I now decided to vary the entertainment. I opened the buttons of his shirt

43

and helped him shrug off the offending garment and then I rolled young Harry across to the left with his shaft still squelching in and out of my cunt, until we had changed positions and I found myself on top of him. I settled myself on his thighs and looked down at the sweet boy whose chest and shoulders were fairly glistening with perspiration. My love channel was now on fire as I rode him like a jockey rides a thoroughbred at the races. Harry's huge cock trembled which I knew heralded an imminent spunking and sure enough he arched his back upwards and his jism shot out with such intensity that I could almost imagine it splashing off the rear wall of my cunt. Indeed, so abundant was his spurting that my thighs were well lathered by his creamy emission as his twitching tadger rubbed itself amorously in a last salute against my sticky pussey.

But a frown appeared on Harry's face as we lay together recovering from this grand exercise in love-making – my fine young man was concerned that I had not spent and I hastened to reassure him that I enjoyed the fuck immensely and that I didn't expect to spend every time. He still looked doubtful so I did my utmost to reassure him that for a girl good sex does not have to involve a fully blown climax. 'Sexual arousal is like a ladder,' I explained, tracing a pattern on his beautiful hairless chest with my fingertip. 'Regretfully, it's one of Nature's quirks that boys shoot up this ladder far quicker than girls. Some girls hide the fact that they haven't been brought off and fake an orgasm but in my opinion it is foolish and unnecessary to pretend as this places a lie at the

44

heart of your relationship.

'We didn't have the time fully to savour the magic of sex – but you have my sworn word that I enjoyed myself just as much as you.'

'I do hope so,' Harry said with a cheeky grin. 'Perhaps next time we'll have more time and we'll come together. Won't that be jolly!'

I clasped my fingers around his flaccid cock and gave it a friendly tug and said, 'Well, we'll see about that, young man. Now you've crossed the Rubicon I think you should have the confidence to find a partner of your own age.'

His face fell but then he kissed me and said with great passion, 'Yes, I know you're right, Jenny, but I'll never forget what happened here this afternoon as long as I live. I'll never be able to thank you enough for your kindness.'

I kissed him lightly on the cheek and replied, 'No thanks are necessary, my dear boy. It was my pleasure to initiate you into manhood.'

We scrambled up and made our way to the pavilion and I saw Osbourne there, standing by the scoreboard which made me think that I should really have left Lockwood Hall by now. But Johnny Lockwood was still out in the field, the junior partner in a heroic stand with Geoffrey Manning against the now tiring attack of the two county bowlers in the Charlatans team. So I scribbled a brief thank-you note to Johnny for all his kindnesses and I also reiterated my promise to contact him early next week before passing it to Harry for safe-keeping.

Osbourne informed me that my clothes had been packed and that Johnny had insisted on filling our tank with petroleum from his own motor-house [private garages were known as motor-houses till the late 1920s – *Editor*] so that we could, God willing, drive all the way non-stop to Chichester. As the weather was so warm, I needed to wear only the light coat Johnny's housekeeper had thoughtfully laid for me on the back seat of the car.

'Very good, Osbourne, we'll leave now,' I told the chauffeur and I instructed him not to drive at a breakneck speed for I never fail to be enchanted by the lovely, rolling countryside in this part of Southern England and haste prevents observation. For I have always maintained that whilst we may well be justified in wanting to get from one place to another as quickly as we can, if the object is to see, to appreciate the beauties of the passing scenery we must be prepared to contribute an amount of imagination which is impossible if we are concerned solely to spend as little time as possible to complete a particular journey.

However, there was little traffic to hold us up and even travelling at a steady speed, we completed our drive in under two hours and it was not yet half past five when we pulled into the driveway of Kathie's house in Polesden Grove which was on the north-western outskirts of the city on the road to Westhampnett. I was very impressed with the Priory which was a charming cottage residence in a quiet and secluded location with well matured gardens. Kathie herself came out to greet me and we embraced warmly for whilst we had kept in touch by letter and although she had briefly visited me in London on a couple of occasions, we had not seen each other since Kathie's old boss Jonathan Claydon had decided to live in California.

'What a delightful place to live,' I exclaimed as I looked around the beautifully laid-out well-timbered grounds.

'Yes, Marcella and I like it very much. We bought the property at a very reasonable price from her Uncle George, who the family always believed to be a confirmed bachelor. But to the family's horror, out of the blue Uncle George upped and married one of his young chamber-maids and the happy couple now live in wedded bliss near Bournemouth.'

A maid came out to show Osbourne where he should take my cases and Kathie said, 'Come and meet Marcella and the two guests who have already arrived. Oh, by the way, we've prepared a room for your driver in the outbuildings over on your right which we converted into the servants' quarters so we've no shortage of bedrooms.'

She escorted me round to the back of the house where a pretty girl with gold-dusted light brown hair, expressive large eyes and blessed with a fine, full feminine figure was talking to two young men who sprang to their feet when Kathie and I approached them.

'Jenny, I want you to meet Marcella Pyecombe who lives with me,' said Kathie and the girl now stood up to shake my hand and said shyly, 'It's a pleasure to meet you, Jenny. Kathie has told me so much about you.'

'Well that's nice to hear, so long as she doesn't have any photographic proof,' I joked and Kathie then introduced Bill Massey and Antony Hammond, the two handsome gentlemen who were like myself guests for the weekend. Mr Massey was perhaps a trifle the taller of the two; he had well-cut features, a determined-looking chin and a pair of greyish-blue eyes that twinkled mischievously as he kissed my hand.

'Delighted to make your acquaintance at last, Miss Everleigh,' said Mr Massey. 'We have several friends in common – Sir Ronnie Dunn, Annabel Quentonne and Raymond Fairbridge to name but three – and they speak so warmly about you that I feel that we know each other even though this is the first time we have actually met.'

'Good heavens, I seem to be the subject of many conversations,' I said lightly turning towards Antony Hammond, who though shorter than Mr Massey, was more broadly built and whose good-looking face enjoyed a healthy, tanned complexion, well set off by the dark wavy hair which curled over his head in picturesque confusion and his luxuriant moustache and neatly trimmed Shakespearean style beard.

'Do we also have friends in common, Mr Hammond?' I asked but he shook his head and replied, 'Alas no, Miss Everleigh, I rarely have the chance to enjoy the delights of the Gay Metropolis as for the last year or so I have spent much of my time in Southern Spain.'

'Oh, how interesting, Mr Hammond, I have been to Madrid and when I was a small girl my parents took me on a cruise in the Mediterranean and I remember that the ship stopped on the Spanish coast for a day at a little Andalusian town called Almunecar.'

He smiled and said, 'I know Almunecar very well, it's a lovely place not far from where I live.'

'You must have a wonderful life there,' said Kathie and he smiled again as he said, 'I enjoy it but life isn't like *Carmen*, you know. Mind, there's sunshine, good food and wine and lots of colour. My home is actually in the Alpujarra, a steep area between the Sierra Nevada and the Sierra de la Contravesa. The people who live there are somewhat isolated in their villages perched up on the hillsides although they are most hospitable where strangers are concerned.'

'What brought you to such a remote area?' enquired Marcella but Bill Massey answered for his friend, 'Tony's life is in ruins.' When we looked aghast he added merrily, 'No, please don't worry, Miss Everleigh, I just mean that Tony is an archaeologist and he is working at the dig headed by the distinguished Oxford University Professor, Sir Meyer Wantman. You may well have read about their findings of some Neolithic tools and weapons there in the newspapers.'

'Yes, I browsed through an article in the *Manchester Guardian* quite recently.

'I'm truly impressed, Mr Hammond,' I said sincerely for my uncle, Lord Camberwell, was a great chum of Professor Wantman and he had told me that the Professor had hand-picked a brilliant young team of workers for this important project. 'Tell me, how long do you plan to stay out there?'

'Only until late November, unless we're lucky enough to make any further significant finds. I'm off back again in two weeks time for my final stint,' he said.

'Do you have any trouble speaking Spanish?' enquired Marcella Pyecombe and again Bill Massey interjected jocularly and chuckled, 'No, but the peasants have trouble understanding him!'

We all laughed and an attractive parlourmaid appeared with glasses of white wine on a tray. 'I hope the wine was nice and cold when you took the bottles from the ice-box, Laura,' said Kathie as the nubile girl offered us the welcome liquid refreshment.

'Oh yes, Miss, I checked carefully before opening one of the bottles,' said Laura, giving a little curtsy before retiring back to the house.

Kathie sighed and commented, 'More likely she checked *after* she opened the bottle and swigged some down, but Laura's a very reliable girl and I don't begrudge her a glass of wine.'

We stayed outside chatting only for another half hour or so and I explained how by a strange coincidence I had met the final guest invited to this little gathering when the honk of a klaxon announced the arrival of Geoffrey Manning himself. He was acquainted with everyone else and I was pleased to hear that thanks to the last wicket stand by himself and Johnny Lockwood, the West Surrey Gentlemen finally vanquished the Charlatans by three wickets.

Then at around seven o'clock we went indoors to dress for dinner which was to be served at eight thirty sharp. A chambermaid had laid out my clothes but I decided to first run a quick warm bath before changing my clothes for the second time that day. And I wondered how the boys and girls would pair off after the meal. As the only female guest, Kathie and Marcella (who I speculated were tribades [lesbians – *Editor*], though from a previous wild night at the Hotel Splendide in Brighton with Barry Gray and other gentlemen I knew that Kathie very much enjoyed occasional visits from Mr Priapus), I would probably be offered first choice of the three cocks on offer. All three gentlemen had their attractions, I mused thoughtfully as I peeled off my clothes and looked at myself in the wardrobe mirror, running my hands over my firm, proud breasts and the little blonde muff of pussey hair which delicately covered my crack.

I slipped on a bathrobe and walked across the landing to the bathroom. The door was slightly ajar and I saw Antony Hammond standing in the bath, soaping himself under the warm, steamy water which was cascading out of the shower-head. He had not heard or seen me enter and he half turned away from me as my eyes quickly focused on his muscular body and his beautifully formed, tight, dimpled buttocks. He turned round slowly, his hands splashing the soap off his face, and I was rewarded by the sight of his thick prick stiffening up into a gigantic boner. He took hold of his tremendous tool and I watched him stroke the shaft up to its full height until it stood stiffly against his belly with the tip reaching his navel.

My nipples began to tremble with excitement at the idea of this lovely juicy cock crashing into my love channel later that evening. I felt myself getting wet as I slipped my hands down between my legs and flicked my fingers around my clitty which was already popping out of its hood and demanding further attention.

But now was not the time to become so fired up and I beat a hasty though noiseless retreat back on to the landing. Marcella sauntered up and said to me, 'Are you waiting to use the bathroom, Jenny? There's another one just over there on the right which is free.'

I thanked her and made my way there. Unlike Antony Hammond, I ensured that the door was closed and the bolt drawn before I began filling the bath with hot water! Anyhow, I bathed and dressed in good time to be downstairs by a quarter past eight for I cannot abide unpunctuality in others and indeed chide myself if I ever keep others waiting.

Dinner was absolutely superb and it was no surprise to later discover that Mrs Hibbert, our excellent cook, was a graduate of the renowned Mrs Angela Bickler's London Academy of Domestic Science. Thankfully Kathie and Marcella were followers of the growing trend to serve less elaborate repasts even though the appetite of a great trencherman like Sir Ronnie Dunn would have been more than satisfied by our splendid meal of cold Vichyssoise soup, Wild Poached Salmon and Salad, Wild Roast Duck With Chestnuts and Orange Sauce served with several green vegetables and potatoes, followed by a variety of fresh fruit including some delicious early peaches from the greenhouse, all washed down with an excellent champagne.

Dear diary, as I have noted before in your pages, champagne is the only alcoholic beverage that is guaranteed to put me in the mood for frolicking and on this warm spring evening, Kathie's Moet et Chandon '03 vintage proved no exception to the rule . . .

Chapter 2

May 17th–18th 1909

No man, however handsome and however wealthy, could ever hope to win my heart except through the force of his own individual personality. I would far rather entertain the rough-hewn prick of a pleasant peasant than the smooth-skinned shaft of a snobbish scion of the aristocracy. (I must remember to copy this sentence in my next letter to cousin Molly as it would do well as a tongue twister at one of her *recherché* afternoon parties!) However, at this particular dinner party I was spoiled for choice for all three gentlemen, Antony Hammond, Geoffrey Manning and Bill Massey were most presentable specimens of the male sex, possessing good looks, beautiful manners, witty speech and easygoing charm.

Frankly, I would not have been averse to inviting all three young men up to my room after dinner as I was feeling rather randy, but this would have been sheer greed and a clear breach of etiquette when there were other pussies waiting to be pleasured. So I decided to home in on Antony (or Tony as he preferred to be known) Hammond and our conversation over dinner became most animated and after a while I knew full well that we would be making love before the night was through.

Reader, you must know how it feels to be sexually attracted to another – there is a real energy which magnetically connects the two of you and the plain truth of the matter was that by the time coffee was served, all I wanted to do was lunge across the table towards Tony who was seated directly opposite me, kiss him long and hard and get my hands down around his thick, delicious cock and ravish him completely – especially when we exchanged heated glances across the table and it was easy to see that Tony was feeling as horny as me!

I was wearing a black evening dress with a low neckline and I calculated that when I leaned forward in a certain way, Tony would be given a clear view of my creamy, ripe breasts. Oooh, just this very thought had my nipples standing erect, swelling against the fine silk of my chemise and I longed for him to kiss and suck them as soon as possible.

So much so, I must confess, that, shielded by the table-cloth, I slipped off my shoes and moved my stockinged foot up between Tony's legs and soon I was able to feel the awesome bulge in his lap and very soon I was stroking the stiff length of his shaft against my toes. He began grinding his groin against my foot but above the table all was calm as I softly declined Laura the maid's offer to refill my coffee cup. Surprisingly Tony too somehow managed to maintain a cool look of stoicism except for the occasional steamy glance he threw across when he judged that no one else was looking, and I am certain that the others never guessed that the poor lad's prick was threatening to burst out of the confines of his trousers.

Tony then showed he possessed a devilish sense of humour for before I knew it he too had wriggled a foot out of a shoe and I smiled as I felt his toes rub themselves against my calf and climb inexorably up my leg. I was so aroused as I felt his sole rub around my crotch that my silky knickers were soon damp with pussey juice.

After dinner, Kathie suggested a walk in the garden and it was noticeable that only Geoffrey Manning accepted with alacrity. Bill Massey and Marcella hung back and Bill's face brightened considerably when Marcella then asked if he would care to see some sketches she had made along the old Roman highway between Billinghurst and Pulborough which had been constructed by Flavius Vespasian, the great general who based his military headquarters in Chichester more than eighteen hundred years ago.

This left Tony and myself alone and he immediately proposed that we retire to either his room or mine. 'Yours, I think,' I murmured and no sooner had we entered the bedroom than we started to tear off each other's clothes. Tony has a fine physique and I admired his lithe, masculine body and noted with satisfaction the size of his cock which though not the largest I had ever seen, was certainly standing up stiffly enough, almost flat up against his lean belly.

I stood there trembling with excitement by the bed in just my silk knickers and garter belt as he took me in his arms and our mouths met in a passionate kiss. The scent of his cologne wafted into my nostrils and his abundant dark chest hair tickled my nipples as he put his hands around my bum cheeks and pressed his throbbing tool against my belly. We sat down on the bed and I wrapped my fingers around the pulsing shaft, gently peeling back the foreskin whilst he worked his hand down to my hairy mound, moving his fingertips between the edges of my soaking slit until sliding them into my juicy honeypot. Then I lowered my head to kiss the majestic purple knob of his throbbing tool. I washed my tongue over the smooth hot helmet which I licked and lapped as he tenderly opened my pussey lips, opening up the passage which was already moistening to a delicious wetness.

'Let's make love, Jenny,' he whispered and I cast my eyes again over Tony's handsome face, warm brown eyes and broad manly chest as he rolled me over on to my back and pressed his rock hard tadger against the yielding lips of my cunney. But then he suddenly pulled back and murmured softly: 'Darling, would you mind very much if I first take you from behind? I have a great fancy for it.'

'Why not?' I replied, turning away from him, and placing my hands on the bed, I pushed out my bottom as I looked back over my shoulder and blew him a loving kiss. Tony smoothed his hands over my rounded buttocks and then pulled them apart. Ah, what a gorgeous feeling of pleasure I experienced as his knob slid into the crevice between my bum cheeks and jiggled around my dripping cunney lips before sliding home.

Despite his long sojourn in Spain (during which he later assured me that his sole nighttime companion was the Widow Thumb and her four fingers), dear Tony Hammond proved to be an experienced master of *l'art de faire l'amour*. His rampant rod filled my cunt and then he withdrew all but an inch before slowly sliding his pulsing prick back in, repeating the squelchy exercise again and again. He gradually increased the tempo as he felt my excitement rising until he was slamming the entire length of his thick cock in and out of my delighted cunt so that his mossy black grove of pubic hair brushed sensuously against the cheeks of my bum at every forward stroke. In no time at all I was bucking and writhing like a crazed beast and Tony had to hold me firmly whilst I shouted, 'Fuck me! Fuck me!' in uninhibited cries of pure, unadulterated lust!

Very soon Tony reached the point of no return and he cried out, 'Jenny, I want to spunk! Can I shoot inside you?'

'Yes! Yes! Go on!' I panted and with a delighted yell he pumped his jet of jism just as I was reaching the heights of a magnificent spend. What a glorious fuck this was, for even though I did not fully climax, I have often found that a fuck from behind is extremely pleasing as, in this position, the cock stimulates the clitty almost without fail.

He pulled his cock out of my cunt and I was delighted to see that Tony's marvellous penis was still semi-erect, waving saucily between his muscular thighs. My body was still afire and so I clambered up on Tony's bed and opened my legs to await my lusty lover. He positioned himself on his knees in front of me and smiled as he looked down on my furry blonde bush with its pink pussey lips pouting through their damp hairy veil. I reached out and placed his hand on my sopping thatch and his fingers splayed my outer lips as with his other hand, he gently ran his thumb down the length of my wet crack. He slid three fingers directly into my love tunnel as my hips rose up to greet the welcome visitors. Then he bent his head forward and I felt his lips pressed against my quim – and I was soon in raptures of delight as Tony found my excitable little clitty and nibbled teasingly on the fleshy morsel.

I clasped my legs around his head as he continued to lick and lap on my engorged love button and I screamed with joy as he brought me off with his tongue. Then after I had released his head I rolled him over on his back and he obeyed with alacrity my command to keep still as I smoothed my hand over his flat tummy and let my finger stray into his curly pubic hair. I licked my lips with gusto when I gazed more closely at Tony's lovely cock which was still not fully erect but which had that delicious heavy look about it. Clasping the warm, wet shaft I slicked my fingers up and down the greasy pole and this had the desired effect! His shaft swelled up to a wonderful stiffness as I uncapped the inviting purple knob and after brushing back some stray hairs from my face, I swooped down and started to lick and kiss the mushroom dome which sent Tony into paroxysms of pleasure. Then I sucked greedily on this tasty lollipop, letting my tongue dwell around the ridge of his helmet, travelling up and down the underside until I sucked in as much of his fat cock as possible between my lips. My head bobbed up and down as I kept my lips taut on his pulsing prick, licking and lapping whilst I palated his shaft with long, rolling sucks and I continued to slurp on his veiny love truncheon until I felt the juices boil up inside his hot, hard shaft. Then I knew he was about to spend; he did so in long powerful spurts which I eagerly swallowed, milking his cock of every last drop of tangy love juice.

To my amazement, his shaft still remained thick and heavy and after I had rubbed it up and down for a minute or so it swelled up again as stiff as could be!

'Goodness gracious, Tony Hammond, does your wonderful cock ever go down?' I giggled as I contemplated his erect, pulsating prick. 'You certainly possess the most extraordinary powers of recovery.'

'Ah, but that's only because I have yet to fuck your darling little notch,' replied the frisky young rascal as he pushed me back and I parted my thighs to await the arrival of Tony's amazing cock. He took hold of his shaft and nudged the knob against my pussey lips and I was already so wet that he entered me easily, sliding his tool

60

deep, deep inside my tingling cunt. At first he moved to and fro with gentle thrusts and just listening to the slurp made by our juices which eased the passage of his prick almost brought me to a spend.

Then Tony began to work up a faster pace, burying his boner inside me with deep, powerful thrusts which mashed my clitty against his pubic bone, which sent a series of thin electric spends crackling through my body. He held us together very still until these spasms ceased and then he started to stroke his cock in and out of my honeypot, penetrating with a lightning force and speed. He managed to keep this up for perhaps thirty seconds and then with one almighty heave he groaned heavily and I felt his body stiffen. Almost immediately my cunney was flooded with a boiling river of hot, sticky spunk and I screamed out in ecstasy as a truly superb spend juddered its way through every fibre of my being and his gushes of juice creamed my cunt in a glorious mutual orgasm.

This time Tony was ready to call a halt to the proceedings and he pulled out his rapidly deflating shaft from my sated pussey. We were both in need of rest after our labours and we cuddled up happily together as we drifted into the welcoming arms of Morpheus.

I was the first to waken and I quietly wriggled out of my lover's embrace and looked at the clock on the bedside table. It was half past one in the morning and I thought it best if I retired to my own bed. So I slipped on my knickers and picked up the rest of my clothes and silently made my barefooted way to the door. I managed to open it without waking Tony and after closing it behind me, I padded across the landing to my own bedroom. I gently opened the door and switched on the electric light.

At first I thought the creaking sound I heard was coming from outside the window – but then I looked across the room and saw to my astonishment that the noise had come from my bed where Marcella was lying stark naked and fast asleep on my eiderdown! Marcella moved slightly and I sat down and stared at this lovely young girl who lay in all her proud glorious nudity on my bed.

She certainly was a gorgeous girl with large snowy breasts, well separated, each looking a little away from each other, each perfectly proportioned and tapering in perfect curves until they came to two rosebud points. Her belly was a smooth plain of whiteness, broad and dimpled, with a sweet little button in the centre and at the base sprouted a thick triangular growth of light brown hair which curled in rich locks round her pussey lips which peeked tantalisingly through their hirsute covering.

Why had this delicious creature come to my room? I walked purposefully across and sat down next to her. It seemed cruel to wake her but surely I had more right than she to sleep here! I pulled down my knickers and lay down next to her on the eiderdown and prepared to close my eyes. The room was very warm as only one window had been left slightly ajar and if I had been on my own I would also have slept on top of the bedclothes so there was no call to disturb Marcella on this account.

But the sight of her delectable breasts just inches from my mouth was so alluring . . . and as poor Oscar Wilde used to say, I can resist anything except temptation! So I carefully moved my head down upon Marcella's lovely large breasts and even in her sleep the beautiful girl sighed with delight as I moved my mouth first to one breast and then to the other, twirling my tongue around the swiftly erecting tawny nipple.

At first she lay passively but then her eyes fluttered open and with a wide smile she whispered, 'Oh Jenny, how nicely you suck my titties! Please go on, I adore it!'

She put her arms round me as I continued to nibble and suck her nips which by now were like two little rubbery stalks as I teased and sucked them up to new heights. Then I let my tongue travel down across her creamy belly and her skin was so soft and smelled so clean that I felt my own pussey beginning to moisten even before I had reached Marcella's dampening mound.

The sweet girl whimpered as I pulled her long legs apart and nuzzled my lips around her curly brown bush. My hands slid underneath her trembling body and clamped themselves around the firm cheeks of her full bottom as my tongue flashed unerringly around the silky pubic thatch. Her cunney lips opened wide as she lifted her backside which enabled me to slip my tongue through the pink edges, licking in long, pistoning strokes between the grooves of her finely developed clitty which, swollen with desire, had popped out of its hood to seek further attention. With a groan of sheer lust, I lost myself in her seductively delicious cunt, lapping with great relish the aromatic juices of Marcella's love channel as she gasped, 'Oooh! Oooh! Oooh! That's simply divine, Jenny! Keep sucking, dearest, eat my pussey! Oh, what a delightful tongue-fuck, how I just love it!'

In truth I needed no urging for my tongue was revelling in her sopping muff, out of which her clitty was now protruding between the pouting lips like a miniature prick. I sucked it into my mouth, rolling the tip of my tongue all around it as Marcella quivered all over and began jerking her body all over the bed and it was hard to keep my tongue lashing her love button as her thighs tightened around my head.

But then she arched her back and with a gigantic shudder she spent profusely, flooding my face with her love juice. I worked my tongue until my jaw ached as the adorable girl again heaved violently and achieved a second tremendous climax.

I gulped down her appetising spend as she sank back on the pillow and the enchanting girl pulled me up across her and we lay panting in each other's arms.

'Let's get under the eiderdown or we might catch cold,' I suggested and she obediently helped me pull out the cover which we spread on top of our warm, perspiring bodies.

Despite our exertions we were no longer sleepy and I asked Marcella whether she solely entertained other girls in her bed or whether, like my cousin Molly Farquhar or Marcella's own partner Kathie McGonagall, she ever varied her diet with the occasional prick. If she ever wanted fucking by a man, I thought to myself, I could heartily recommend the seasoned tool of Antony Hammond which I was sure would cream her cunney to great effect.

'Oh yes, I enjoy a nice thick cock now and then, although I was not particularly bothered when Kathie said to me before dinner that she had a yen to be fucked by Bill Massey and Geoffrey Manning simultaneously,' said Marcella carelessly and she added, 'I watched whilst Kathie sucked Bill's tool whilst Geoffrey fucked her but when the two gentlemen changed positions I left to come up here and wait for you. I guessed that you would be with Tony Hammond. He's a very good fuck, isn't he? And I've never known a man like Tony who can keep his cock so stiff after spending.'

'Yes, it's quite remarkable, but I'm a little surprised that he's had you already. You couldn't have had much time before dinner.' I remarked, tracing a circle round her saucer-shaped dark areolae which so sensuously set off her large nipples.

'Oh yes, Tony arrived two days ago and during the days he helped us with the stocktaking in the bookshop. Last night I asked him to fuck me and I must say that I was very impressed with his abilities. Weren't you?'

I agreed that Tony's technique was of the highest quality and I asked Marcella if this were the first time she had sampled the good-looking young chap's cock.

'No, we made love when I went up to London for Deborah Paxford's coming-out party about two years ago. Funnily enough Geoffrey Manning was also there, as it happens, and I suppose it was because of his antics that Tony and I finished up in bed together,' she said reflectively.

'It sounds like quite a wild party,' I commented as I opened my legs to allow her hand to rub my pussey as she talked. 'Deborah invited me as well but as the very next day I was off to Australia [*see Jenny Everleigh 9: Call That A Boomerang – Editor*] I was unable to go.'

'Oh, it was very enjoyable but it wasn't a fast affair at all,' said Marcella, 'but what happened was that I had two blank spaces on my dance card and I wandered out into the garden for a walk. But as I neared the summerhouse at the far end of the garden I thought I heard the voice of my close friend Georgina Lucas saying, "Geoffrey my sweetheart, you must stop it, you're making me far too randy and we can hardly make love here."

'Now I know I should not have eavesdropped but my curiosity was aroused so I crept closer and looked in to see just what was happening. Well, the two of them were standing together in the centre of the summerhouse. Their arms were clasped around each other and they were staring in each other's eyes.

' "But Georgie, my pet," Geoffrey wailed pitiably, "we haven't made love for a full two weeks. I'm bursting for a fuck! Here, feel for yourself!" And as I stood there he ripped open his trousers and pulled out his immense stiff cock. "Here, feel how hard it is, all ready to slide into your juicy pussey."

'He placed her hand round his thick shaft and she worked her fingers up and down it as their lips met in a fervent clinging kiss and Geoffrey's arms slid down behind her and he brazenly pulled up her dress to the waist, exposing Georgina's naked buttocks because the naughty girl wasn't wearing any underclothes! He clutched her rounded bum cheeks as she continued to frig his cock as they lurched across to a couch-like seat and sank down upon it – but now as her legs fell apart, Geoffrey's hand came from behind her and slid into her fully exposed cunt.

'Geoffrey threw up her dress even further until she was naked from her breasts to the tops of her stockings which were held up solely by frilly red garters and Georgina rotated her bum round on the seat as he toyed with the thick black curls and dipped his fingertip into the crimson gap of her cunney which peaked out so invitingly whilst she continued to rub his twitching tool in a quick up and down motion.

'Then he suddenly dropped to his knees between hers and for a moment I was given an unhindered view of her pretty cunt which gaped open, a trickle of love juice already dripping down her thighs. But as I stared at her pouting cunney, Geoffrey plunged his face into the forest of black hair and kissed and tongued her cunney in a veritable frenzy of passion. Georgina's head rolled from side to side and tiny moans escaped from her lips as her hands came down on his head and he lifted her thighs to his shoulders and wrapped his arms about her waist. Her hips jerked violently and with a cry of "Oh, My God!" on her lips she shivered all over and made no resistance as Geoffrey disengaged his head from between her thighs. Now she lay down on the couch with her legs apart as he clambered over her, his trousers and drawers down to his knees and his huge cock waving in the air like a bar of iron.

'I ran my tongue over my lips as she grasped hold of this veiny love shaft and placed the uncapped knob against her pussey lips. Then with his hands on her hips, Geoffrey pushed himself forward, driving his rampant rammer deep inside the gleaming, wet crack of her cunney and Georgina's legs came up around his back whilst her arms circled his neck as they swayed backwards and forwards in frenetic rhythm.

'Watching this passionate fuck made my own pussey very damp as I thought how nice it would be to feel a long, thick peg of throbbing cock ease its way slowly between the soft and clinging walls of my own sopping slit. My hands strayed down to rub my pussey through the fine silk material of my dress but then I heard the sound of footsteps behind me. I turned round and who should be walking down the garden path but Tony Hammond! "Hello there, Miss Pyecombe," he called out. "I was looking everywhere for you. We have the next dance, you know, and it will be starting any minute now."

'He came up to me and said, "What brings you out here? is it –" and then he broke off as he

68

noticed what was going on behind me. The horny pair had finished fucking but Geoffrey was sitting on the couch and Georgina was on her knees in front of him lustily sucking his glistening white shaft, her dark tresses spreading along his thighs as he jerked his hips upwards to stuff as much of his throbbing column as he could inside her soft mouth.

' "I say," breathed Tony and stood stock still for a moment and I could see a large bulge form between his legs. Then he took a few deep breaths and with an effort, Tony collected his thoughts as he mopped his brow. 'Miss Pycombe, shall we go back inside for our waltz?" he asked politely, for being a gentleman he made no comment upon what was taking place before his very eyes in the summerhouse.

'I accepted his invitation and after our dance I suggested to him that if he liked, we could plead a trifling headache to our partners for the next dance and then meet upstairs in one of Lord Paxford's many private rooms on the first floor. "What a splendid idea, Miss Pyecombe," he murmured, his liquid eyes looking sensuously into mine as he escorted me off the dance-floor at the end of the ballroom far from the madding crowd.

' "My name's Marcella," I smiled and added, "and my friends *don't* call me Marcie." He chuckled and said, "And my name's Anthony but I don't mind my friends calling me Tony."

'We each made our way upstairs on our own and unfortunately the first door I opened was occupied by our hostess who was engaged in an ardent bare-breasted embrace with the Honourable Alexander Ross. "So sorry, Debbie," I muttered and shut the door firmly on the startled pair. I looked back and saw that Tony was beckoning me from the other side of the corridor and when I reached him he opened the door to the perfect place for love-making. The room had a table upon which there was a tray of drinks including an ice bucket with a bottle of champagne inside it and there was also a very inviting red velvet sofa upon which I sat down whilst Tony locked the door behind us.

' "Should we be in here?" I queried as he opened the bottle of champagne. "Probably not," he replied cheerfully, "but, what the heck, let's enjoy ourselves, after all, this is Debbie Paxford's coming-out party when all is said and done."

'Well, this was true enough and Debbie's breasts were certainly coming out of their confines in the hands of the Honourable Mr Ross across the corridor and I decided to follow her example. We drank some champagne but we were both feeling frisky already and very soon we were kissing and canoodling on the sofa. I was wearing a decolleté dress which exposed a daring amount of bosom and it took only a few moments before Tony was passing his lips over my naked breasts, licking and lapping my big red titties in great style.

'Meanwhile I leaned forward and let the palm of my hand glide over the huge bulge in Tony's crotch. He groaned as I felt his cock pulse through the material of his black evening trousers. "Aaah, I'll do myself an injury if l don't take my prick out,

Marcella, or at least I'll spunk inside my drawers," he whispered fiercely.

' "We'd better release Mr Cock then," I smiled and I unbuttoned his flies and pulled out his swollen shaft. I thought it a good specimen with a large ruby crown and I wrapped my fingers around the glowing pole and gave the ivory column a little preliminary tug as he raised my head upwards and closer to his own and our lips closed upon each other's as we melted away into a most arduous kiss.

'We fell back together and our lips remained fastened together. Tony carefully unbuttoned my dress and somehow I managed to wriggle out of it. He helped me pull off my chemise and I lifted my bottom as he tugged down my knickers with a certain urgent roughness which I did not find displeasing and then he swiftly divested himself of all his clothing and we were both completely nude. Now his hand was working its way up my thigh inexorably towards my groin and his long fingers felt lovely as they toyed with my burning cunney; I lay back and waited expectantly for the *pièce de résistance* and I was not to be disappointed when I felt the smooth helmet of his cock pushing down against my pussey lips and I murmured, "That's nice," as he continued to press forward into my wetness.

'For a moment our eyes locked together and then, with a heartfelt sigh, he inserted an inch or two of his lovely thick prick inside my clinging cunt. Our lips meshed together and I wriggled my arse to obtain more of this meaty morsel. Tony understood my need and clutching my naked bum cheeks, he embedded his sturdy shaft down to the very root and in some magical way my little cunney somehow expanded itself to receive this plump but extremely welcome visitor.

'I could not speak. I was filled by him. His thick prick slid juicily in and out of my clinging cunney and his big balls hung in their hairy sack, swinging against my bum as with a powerful jolt of his loins, he inserted the full length of his hard, smooth shaft inside me – and then the young scamp teased me by taking out all but the very tip of his knob which made me beg for its immediate return! I know that some measure of modesty should be present at all times even during those first ecstatic moments of erotic bliss but I don't mind confessing that I cried out unashamedly for Tony Hammond to thrust his cock back into my juicy crack.

'Now we started to fuck in joyful unison, our bottoms heaving together as he slewed his stalwart shaft in and out of my luscious cunt. 'Oh, Marcella, what a delicious pussey you have,' he gasped as he pistoned his prick to and fro. ''How tightly it clasps my cock! That's the way, dearest, work your bum up and down in time with me – but not too much or I will spunk too quickly!''

'Fortunately we were uninterrupted during this voluptuous joust, which was just as well for the two of us were totally lost in that sensual world where fulfilment is all and frankly even if Debbie's uncle, the Rural Dean of Stroud, had entered the room, I doubt if we would have taken a blind bit of notice of the distinguished cleric.

'Tony's penis slicked in and out of my cunt,

pistoning back and forth and I gloried in each powerful stroke as my own juices sprinkled his ballsack. Cupped now upon his broad palms, the tight cheeks of my backside savagely rotated as his lusty tool continued to ram home at an ever-increasing pace. I felt the first stirrings of my spend and I cried out, "I'm almost there! I'm coming, Tony, I'm coming! A-h-r-e! Empty your balls in my cunney, you naughty big-cocked boy!"

'And with his face buried in my neck and his hot breath warming my shoulder I could feel that he too was about to climb the highest peaks of pleasure. Although we might both have preferred this marvellous fuck to last, Nature was not to be denied and we were very soon lost in the throes of a glorious mutual spend and my cunney was awash with Tony's copious emission of frothy white sperm as my cunney exploded around his throbbing prick.

'We lay panting with exhaustion in a rather undignified heap of limbs and I complimented the dear lad on his prowess, for I rarely fail to praise a good lover. Incidentally, though I may lack the necessary information for a truly scientific appraisal, my own empiric research leads me to believe that the further north one travels, the thicker the pricks. Tony Hammond was an exception to this rule but I have found that Scottish cocks appear to be slightly bulkier. Not that this matters overmuch, for as our American friends say, "It isn't the size of the ship that counts, it's the motion of the ocean."

'Be that as it may, we dressed hastily for we did

not exactly care to explain where we had been and fortune was with us for we were not missed by any of the other guests though, rather amusingly, we met Debbie and Alexander coming out of their bedroom where they had obviously also been enjoying themselves in a similar fashion. Tony escorted me home in a Prestoncrest Carriage [a private motor-car service used by members of Society who knew that Prestoncrest drivers were sworn to secrecy about who was being transported to which destination and several illicit liaisons flourished in the black Prestoncrest Lanchester vehicles – *Editor*] and we engaged in a further splendid fuck in my house before he left as the first rays of dawn were breaking through the sky.'

Now of course her recitation of this libidinous anecdote had made my cunney moisten, especially as Marcella had been tickling my pussey all the while and her busy fingers now made my heartbeat quicken and my whole body tremble with desire. I felt quite light-headed as she began to take all the liberties she desired with me, kissing and sucking my curvaceous full breasts, frigging my erect little clitty and brazenly handling the soft cheeks of my fleshy bum, squeezing and pinching them as I writhed under her lascivious touch. When she eased a finger into my dampening slit, I sighed and raised my backside to enjoy the delicious sensations to the utmost. Now her finger was joined by a second and then a third as she finger-fucked me so expertly that I went off time and again.

Marcella now moved up over me and, still

keeping her wicked fingers embedded in my cunt, kissed me fervently on the mouth. Her velvet tongue slithered between my lips to make contact as her fingers moved to plunge in and out of my juicy love channel. Then the naughty minx left off her manual stimulation and replaced her fingers with her tongue as she grasped my bum cheeks one in each hand, and dropped her face between my legs, her lips pressed against the soft yielding flesh, probing and coaxing the petals of my cunt to open like a flower.

She then arranged me so that I was lying on my back and partly on my right side. My right leg was out almost straight, my left one drawn up, the heel of this foot being hooked behind her neck. Her left cheek rested on my right thigh, her left arm was under me and clasped about my waist, her right hand resting upon and toying with my breasts. Propped up against the pillows, I was in a good position to gaze down on the pretty girl as her lips pressed the gentlest of kisses on my cunt, now and then letting the tip of her tongue glide along between the lips.

Oh, but Marcella was so wicked! Time and again she felt me approach a spend she would stop, look into my eyes and wait until the gathered forces of an orgasm melted away. But then she moved her body across me so that we were entwined together in the lewdest of *soixante neufs*. She carefully lowered her bum on to my face until her juicy crack was almost touching my lips and I parted her buttocks and licked and lapped around her sweet snatch as she glued her mouth to my own dripping pussey, sucking and nipping at the tender clitty in much the same way as I was working on her.

We sighed and moaned in unison as we lay there with our mouths firmly pressed against each other's pussey. I was tonguing deep inside Marcella's cute little cunt and her cunney juices were flowing freely whilst her clitty had grown quite enormous with all this erotic love-play. I nipped her clitty as she in turn sucked up the love liquid which was pouring from my own pussey, licking and lapping with great ardour.

'Aaaah! Aaaah! Pull my clitty and make me spend!' I gasped and the gorgeous girl wrenched her mouth away from my sopping muff and replaced it with a further session of frigging by her long, tapering fingers; she frigged my swollen clitty so superbly that my body began thrashing around underneath her in a frenzied animalistic ecstasy – and when she slid a cunning finger into my bottom-hole I thought I would fairly explode as gigantic spasms of lustful thrills ran through my body, culminating in a tremendous orgasmic spend.

'Now do the same for me please, darling,' she said, scrunching her bottom on my face. Nothing loath, I pushed my mouth hard up against her, moving my entire head back and forth as I nuzzled my lips between her pink cunney lips from which her love juice was oozing in a veritable rivulet as I sucked upon her nut-hard clitty, flicking my tongue in and out of her hairy quim, noisily slurping the juices from her cute little cunt as her yelps of joy filled the night air with the sounds and scent of sexual satisfaction.

76

I judged that Marcella's orgasm was building up and I worked my tongue even harder whilst at the same time I dipped my forefinger inside her cunney, deeper and deeper until she finally screamed with delight as she achieved her spend in waves of pure, raw energy that coursed out from her sated cunt.

Marcella slumped down on top of me though her body weight caused me little discomfort. But like me she looked up in surprise when we heard the rattle of a key and in the open doorway stood the figure of Mr Massey. I was dumbfounded but Marcella snapped, 'Well come in, Bill, don't just stand there like the proverbial spare prick at a wedding.'

'I'd love to, so long as I am not *persona non grata*,' he replied with a slight smile. 'After all, remember you did decline my invitation to come up to my room earlier this evening.'

'I know, and perhaps I should apologise as I may have led you to believe otherwise, but I just wasn't in the mood,' said Marcella, 'but Jenny Everleigh has made my blood boil and as long as she doesn't mind, you're very welcome to join us.'

He looked enquiringly at me and I pulled Marcella's bum up from my lips and turning my face towards him I said, 'Do join us, Bill, don't be shy. I'm sure that Marcella and I can always find room for a trusty stiff cock.'

'Yes, of course we can,' Marcella added gaily. 'Just shut the door behind you and take off your clothes, Bill. Then come and join us on the bed.'

With commendable alacrity, Bill Massey did as

he was told, shedding his garments immediately and, even more commendably, he asked what *our* pleasure might be as he stood by the bed, the shaft of his proud prick cupped in his right hand.

Marcella was also impressed by Bill's gallantry and as she slid off me she said, 'This looks like a succulent cock, Jenny. Shall we see if it tastes as good as it looks?'

'By all means,' I answered and we pulled Bill down on the bed and Marcella knelt by his left thigh and I knelt by his right as we took turns to lick his hot, rock-hard staff. Then Marcella gobbled the knob and the top inch or so of his shaft whilst I kissed and lapped around his hairy ballsack. Then we changed places and I sucked his cock, savouring the salty flavour of his truncheon as he thrust the slippery rod deeper into my mouth and I helped him by sliding my lips as far down the shaft as possible, feeling his wiry pubic hair tickling my nose as I inhaled its fragrant perspiration. He spent very quickly and I swallowed his creamy spunk in great gulps, pulling him hard into my mouth as he delivered the contents of his palpitating balls, filling my mouth with his frothy emission and I sucked on his cock until his penis began to shrink back to flaccidity.

But Marcella's blood was up and she murmured thoughtfully, 'I think there is still some life here,' and she took Bill's cock in her hands and sure enough by rubbing up the shaft it soon swelled up as hard, high and handsome as before.

Bill cleared his throat and said, 'May I now please fuck one of you two lovely girls?'

'Of course you may,' I said, 'although to be fair, I think you should fuck Marcella first as her need is greater than mine.'

He nodded and said, 'In that case, Jenny, would you have a pot of cold cream on your dressing-table? If so, I would be obliged if I could have some.'

I heaved myself out of bed and fetched him the small jar he had requested and he dipped his hand inside and applied a liberal amount of cold cream to his erect cock.

'Oh Bill,' said Marcella falteringly as she eyed his glistening tool, 'do you want to fuck my bottom? I've never had a prick up my bum before.'

'Don't worry, my dear, I won't hurt you,' he replied cheerfully. 'The rear dimple can be a most delightful channel of bliss and if this is to be your first time, I hope that it will open up your senses to a ravishment of which you have hitherto had no conception. Although strictly speaking it is against the law [it was only in 1861 that the death penalty for anal intercourse was repealed though the last recorded execution was in 1836 – *Editor*], I have it on the highest medical authority that the practice is harmless. [Modern medical opinion would agree, so long as the man takes matters at a gentle pace, though there is a danger that germs can be passed from the back to the front passage and cause a vaginal infection – *Editor*].

'Also, you won't have to worry about becoming *enceinte* from being fucked this way and you can honestly tell your current beau that you have saved your pussey solely for his delectation,' he added as he climbed on to the bed and, as instructed, Marcella lay down on her elbows with her buttocks pushed firmly upwards whilst Bill angled her legs further apart to afford himself a better view of her wrinkled brown rosette; then he nudged his knob in between her rolling bum cheeks.

'Ow! Ow! This isn't much fun,' she cried but Bill pushed on with his hands gripping her hips and her sphincter muscle gradually relaxed and she began to enjoy the experience, especially when I reached down and began frigging her cunney. His thick cock now bounced inside her tight sheath as if spring-loaded and he now plunged it easily to and fro, pumping away like the piston of a steam-engine. Bill pulled Marcella's bum cheeks further apart and her bottom now jerked in time with Bill's rhythmic fucking. Then with a low grown he spent, jetting a fountain of foamy jism inside her puckered bum-hole and he withdrew his still semi-stiff cock with an audible 'pop'.

'There, I do hope that you enjoyed it?' Bill panted and Marcella blew out her cheeks as she replied: 'Yes, after the initial discomfort it was very nice, but I still prefer a girl's sweet lips sucking my cunney above all other sensual joys.'

He looked somewhat disappointed but I said, 'Ah well, different strokes for different folks, Bill, you should know the truth of that old maxim. Perhaps like me, your own personal preference is for a good old-fashioned fuck, yet there are some men – Sir Robert Cripps or General Searle to name but two – who swear that nothing can beat the rich red lips of a pretty girl clamped round their cocks.'

And on that note, we ended this engagement for I now said farewell to Bill and Marcella who, after gathering up their clothes, tip-toed naked out of my room though I had a shrewd suspicion that Marcella's pussey would be filled by Bill's sizeable love truncheon before daybreak. But at last lying alone in my bed, I swiftly fell into a deep sleep.

May 18th, 1909 (continued)

Well, I may have slept deeply, diary, yet despite the many diversions of the previous evening, I nevertheless woke soon after dawn, disturbed perhaps by the sounds of the country for the calls of wild birds, the lowing of cattle and the contented clucking of hens are never heard in the vicinity of Belgravia or Mayfair.

So, shortly after six o'clock I had bathed and dressed and as the sun was already blazing in the early morning sky, I decided to wander round the gardens. However, when I neared the outbuildings which served as quarters for Kathie and Marcella's servants, I imagined that I could hear the singularly unique sounds of a coupling. Surely, I was mistaken, I said to myself, as I walked quietly round to the side of the building from where the whimpers and sighs of passion were coming, and I popped my head round the corner to see for myself whether my own recent intimate adventures had affected my mental judgement.

Well, I am pleased to note that my initial thoughts were absolutely right! It took only a swift glance to confirm that the sounds were of a passionate coupling and the pair involved were none other than my driver Herbert Osbourne and Laura, the attractive parlourmaid who had served wine to the guests soon after my arrival the previous afternoon!

The two of them were writhing half-naked on a couple of blankets which had probably been filched from the laundry and I watched with mounting interest as the nubile girl pulled her chemise over her head revealing as the material fell away, her large milky-white breasts; she touched them lightly, her fingers brushing the nipples and then passing upwards to unloosen her hair. This movement of Laura's arms made her breasts lift with the flushed pink circle which ran around each nipple, heightening its colour and framing each erect little teat at its centre. The two lovely orbs of her ripe young bosoms gently bumped together as Laura now lowered her arms again and she then wriggled out of her white cotton knickers and ran her hand through her curly auburn triangle of pussey hair.

'Well, Herbert, you've seen the merchandise displayed – are you in the market to make a purchase? I'll warn you now that there are no credit terms and to buy means that you'll have to make a deposit, the more substantial the better! Or shall I just wrap the goods up again?' Laura said with a cheeky giggle.

'Oh, I'll make a deposit, have no fear,' growled my, driver who whilst she was speaking had divested himself of all his clothing and displayed his thick, pulsating prick which Laura rubbed up and down – and what an immense cock my driver possessed for Laura could no longer span it with her fingers.

I watched with growing interest as Laura's head dived down to kiss the purple uncapped helmet of Osbourne's enormous cock as she played with his prick – coyly at first, sliding her hand up and down the blue-veined shaft – and then with a downward lunge she plunged it far into her mouth and started to suck it with all her might. Osbourne gave a little gasp and he clutched her head in his hands as her lips bobbed up and down, cramming more and more of his thick prick until she must have felt the tip of his knob touch the back of her throat, for she gagged for a moment or two and was forced to ease out an inch or so of his shaft between her wide-stretched lips.

Feeling her warm, wet lips caress his cock made Osbourne's back arch in ecstasy. 'Yes, yes, suck my cock, Laura, you naughty girl!' he grunted as she slurped happily away, now lapping her wet tongue around the 'eye' to suck up his pre-spend before gobbling furiously on his twitching tool. Then a hoarse groan from Osbourne signalled that he was about to spend and Laura caressed his balls as he shot what must have been a copious emission into her mouth for, despite her frenzied attempts to swallow all his creamy jism, some of the sticky spunk rolled down her chin and on to the blanket.

I was pleased to see that Osbourne was ready

to repay the precocious girl for his sucking off by returning the compliment in the best way possible even though Laura had milked his penis so well that it now hung flabbily over his thigh. He pushed the parlourmaid down on her back and slid his hands under her legs to fondle her bare bottom whilst he pressed his lips to her inviting red titties which he kissed, sucked and nipped in fine style. Then he released his hands from her bum cheeks and placed them on her thighs which he parted as he kissed the curly brown tufts of pussey hair whilst his hands sped upward, tweaking and rubbing her engorged nipples with his fingers. She opened her legs wider and fully exposed her puffy cunney lips which now pouted deliciously from the silky brown bush of pussey hair.

Although I could not actually see his tongue flash along the lips of her cunney, Osbourne must obviously have known how to tease a clitty for it was clear that he was pleasuring the sumptuous young girl's cunt for˙she shivered all over as he palated her pussey and she called out, "Enough! Enough! Put it in!' she ordered and with his stiff shaft waggling like a flagpole in the wind, Osbourne answered his call and clambered upon her rich, ample curves. A moan from them both signalled that he must have found the target immediately and their lips met as Laura jerked her lovely bottom up and down so as to absorb as much of his palpitating prick as possible.

He began pumping his prick in and out of her juicy furrow with long, slow strokes and then he speeded up the pace and I distinctly heard his balls crack against her bottom as they trashed away. Laura was thoroughly enjoying being fucked and I heard her mutter fiercely, 'Go on, Herbert, what a big, fat cock you have! Can you feel my cunney muscles gripping your shaft as it slides in and out? Go on, you rascal, crack away now!'

Osbourne did as he was told and I could see that her crack had received all of his cock and she twisted her legs to keep his rampant rod clenched inside her cunt as she sensuously rotated her hips as the willing chauffeur vigorously heaved his buttocks and Laura's bum moved in time with his, answering his lunges with upward thrusts of her own.

'I'm coming, I'm coming, go faster, faster!' she howled and he grunted a wordless reply as his balls smacked against her bum with every powerful stroke. His body tensed and then with a savage shudder he impelled the first gush of spunk inside her love channel.

'Aaah! Aaah! Here I go, do more, more!' she screamed out as she clawed at his back as the virile driver pumped spurt after spurt of creamy spray into her welcoming cunney.

They lay still on the blankets for a few moments until Laura sat up and said, 'Oh Herbert, that was the best fuck I've had for weeks! There aren't many men I fancy round here and though the curate comes round every Thursday to have his cock sucked, I only get fucked twice a month at best by an occasional visitor. Perhaps we can have another fuck this afternoon though because Miss Kathie told me last night that she plans to take her guests out for a walk around Chichester after luncheon so I'm sure to have some time off.'

'I'd love to oblige but I'll have to drive them to Chichester, won't I,' said Osbourne gloomily, 'and it's odds-on that I'll have to wait while they stroll round the town.

'Mind, Miss Jenny is no great walker and I wouldn't be surprised if we come back quite early,' he added, his face brightening up as he put on his drawers. 'It's strange really, but her parents are always off hiking around the country and you might have heard of her uncle, Sir Bonnington Everleigh is a famous mountaineer, but Miss Jenny has never been a great one for Shanks's Pony.'

'Yet she has a lovely figure. I suppose she takes her exercise in some other way,' said Laura and to my extreme displeasure, Osbourne guffawed and said, 'I'll bet she does! Why, the men buzz around her like flies and I'm sure she knows what's what, if you get my drift.'

Well, they do say listeners never hear good of themselves though my anger was softened when he added, 'Mind, I don't blame them one little bit. After all, she's a beautiful girl from a rich family and she has the sweetest nature. All Mr and Mrs Everleigh's staff think the world of Miss Jenny and I do too.' Then he proceeded to tell Laura about how we were held up on the journey down to Chichester because he had forgotten to load the toolbox in the car. And he concluded, 'I thought I might have to look around for another job, but Miss Jenny took it all in her stride even though she was rightly put out by the inconvenience.'

My ears were beginning to burn but thankfully Laura changed the subject and as she folded up the blankets she remarked, 'I'll have to put these in the wash, Herbert. My, look how stained this one is from our spendings.'

At this point I left the naughty twosome and walked quietly back to the house. I went into the library and read a magazine until Geoffrey and Kathie came down together at about half past seven. 'You're an early bird,' said Kathie as we went into the dining-room. 'Did you sleep well?'

'Yes, thank you,' I said and I suddenly realised that despite our sumptuous repast last night, I was feeling very hungry and tucked in to a hearty meal. Despite the fact that we were in the country, Kathie's cook had laid out a full breakfast. On one sideboard there was a row of silver dishes, kept hot by spirit lamps and there were scrambled eggs, bacon, sausages, devilled kidneys and poached haddock and on the other was a selection of cold meats – pressed beef, ham and tongue – whilst a side-table was heaped with apples, oranges, peaches and nectarines. Laura stood by a large jug of freshly squeezed orange juice and there were pots of coffee and tea as well as plates of bread, rolls and toast. I looked at her closely but from her impassive face one would hardly have realised that she had recently been engaged in a passionate coupling on the grass although her clear skin and bright, shining eyes showed something that I have always maintained, namely that a splendid fuck in the morning sets you up nicely for the rest of the day.

Along with the others I spent a lazy morning

reading the newspapers and doing nothing more strenuous than playing ping-pong [table-tennis – *Editor*] with Geoffrey, Bill and Marcella in the games room, although I also took the opportunity of looking through some mail which had arrived for me in London the previous day but which I had not yet opened, let alone answered.

There was only one letter of any importance and that was from Johnny Oaklands, one of my oldest and closest friends [just how close may be gauged from *Jenny Everleigh 4: The Secret Diaries – Editor*] who was now living on his family's grand country estate near Porlock in North Devon. Johnny had studied law but after he had qualified, although he had been invited to take up a position at the high-ranking Society solicitors Godfrey and Godfrey, he declined to take up the opportunity, saying that he preferred a peaceful country life to the noise and bustle of London. And since the tragic death of his poor Papa, Sir Garfield Oaklands, in a road accident during a motoring holiday three years ago, Johnny has been fully occupied with his duties as lord of the manor and squire of the village of Allendale.

Indeed, I had not heard from Johnny for several weeks even though I had sent him a brief letter in mid-April whilst I was spending a week in Paris at Count Gewirtz's mansion on the Rue de la Paix. So I was genuinely delighted to see his handwriting on the envelope which I tore open and soon began to giggle when I started to read his letter which I am sure he will not mind, dear diary, being reproduced in your pages:

Dearest Jenny,

Please forgive my poor manners in not replying more promptly to your newsy letter from Paris. How is the Count? Really, his prick should drop off from overuse if there were any justice in the world. I read in the Oyster *recently that these days the old reprobate is fucking Lady Sarah Jane Ethelbridge though he is still very friendly with Princess Marussa of Samarkand and according to the Parisian correspondent of the* Oyster, *the randy old sod fucks the two of them, one after the other after dinner every Thursday night, the lucky so-and-so!*

Truth to tell, Jenny, I must confess to being more than a little envious of the Count, for the old goat always seems to have a never-ending stream of pretty girls at his beck and call. As for me, my only solace has been the so-called solitary vice though what harm can there be in pulling your pud? It's free, quick and easy though I wouldn't go as far as the jokester from our Embassy in Siam who penned that funny limerick:

> *There once was a man of high station*
> *Attached to the British legation*
>   *He loved being fucked*
>   *And adored being sucked*
> *But he revelled in pure masturbation!*

Still, whilst frigging has its compensations and is far, far better than celibacy, it cannot really rival a damn good fuck and stuck down here in the country, that's something I've been without for the last three months. Last night I thought about you and the marvellous fucking we enjoyed when you were living at your Aunt

Portia's house in Kensington whilst your parents were out in Greece. Do you remember those delicious couplings we enjoyed on your visits to my lodgings in Albion Square?

I'll never forget the time you came round after attending a spring ball at Lord and Lady Hartmouth's. I was burning the midnight oil cramming for my final Bar examinations when I was disturbed by a knock on the front door which I answered myself because I had given my servant the night off. I opened the door and who should be standing there but the beautiful Jenny Everleigh herself in all her glory.

'Hello, Johnny,' you said sweetly, giving me a luscious kiss on my cheek.

'I've come to see how you are progressing with your studies. I can't help with your revision, my darling, but I thought I might help to clear your brain for a while before you tackle some more beastly work.'

I escorted you in and my heart began to pound when I helped you of with your coat and I saw your beautifully rounded breasts which were only partially covered by a daring turquoise gown. We were barely inside the hall when we exchanged a burning kiss and I murmured, 'How lovely to see you, Jenny, what a wonderful surprise,' and all thoughts of further study fled from my mind as your hand slipped down between us to rub your palm deliciously over my fast-stiffening shaft.

We wasted no further time and I picked you up in my arms and carried you to my bedroom where we tore off our clothes. We stood naked in each other's arms as my lips travelled down from your pretty face to your proud, jutting breasts. Then we fell back on the bed and I sucked gently on your erect red titties, going from one to another and licking everything in between.

'Master, John, you need taking in hand,' you said with a giggle as you wrapped your long, slender fingers around my bursting cock. Then your full, sensuous lips opened wide and moved slowly down to my rigid prick, licking, lapping, sucking, moving faster as your hands caressed my hairy balls. Meanwhile I worked my body round until my face was between your legs and I could pay homage to your fluffy blonde bush, working my tongue all along the edges of your wet slit, probing your dainty cunney as you ground your silky snatch against my mouth and sucked lustily on my cock, twirling your tongue all over my big rounded bell end.

How fiercely the sperm boiled up in my balls! I felt my shaft tensing itself for a powerful emission and I spurted a fountain of frothy white love cream into your throat, lapping your cunney juice as your pussey also exploded into the sweet agonies of a spend.

At this stage I did not finish reading Johnny's letter for I was now aware that someone was breathing heavily in front of my chair. I glanced up and saw the figure of Bill Massey whose blue eyes twinkled as he said to me, 'Forgive me for disturbing you, Jenny, but I could not help noticing that the *billet doux* you are reading has certainly fired your imagination.'

'Now what made you come to that conclusion?' I asked and Bill looked around him to ensure that he would not be overheard.

'Well, your hand strayed down to your lap whilst you were reading and began rubbing your pussey,' he grinned, 'so one hardly needs to be a Sherlock Holmes to realise that the letter was more than a trade circular or an epistle from your

Auntie Pamela.'

I smiled as the dear man slipped his arm around my waist and drew me close to him so that he could nibble my ear.

'We really shouldn't do this,' I protested weakly as he took me tenderly in his arms and inserted his hands inside my blouse and let his finger rove around my hardening nipples. Our lips met and we eased ourselves down on to the rich Persian carpet which was almost as comfortable as a mattress, especially when Bill placed a cushion under my head.

'Bill, stop this, someone might come in,' I muttered but he shook his head and whispered that he had locked the door behind him after seeing me play with my pussey – which had greatly aroused him.

Slipping off his jacket, I began to unbutton his trousers and turning them down, my eager hands wandered under his shirt, feeling the firmness of the rounded contours of his buttocks and I could hardly fail to notice the bulge in his drawers which made the white linen stand out. I slid my hand inside the slit and grasped hold of his massive love truncheon which stood up magnificently from the mass of curly dark pubic hair at the root of his prick. I pulled my hand up and down the hot, smooth-skinned shaft as we divested ourselves of our remaining garments and our nude bodies threshed wildly away on the carpet. Then he laid me down and parted my thighs to expose my pink pussey lips and his head shot between my legs and I wrapped my thighs around it as his lips fastened on to my cunt. His deft fingers parted my cunney lips and he licked my juicy crack from top to bottom. I writhed in ecstasy as he now penetrated my soaking quim with his tongue and he sucked in my clitty between his lips. He mashed it hard as his fingers darted in and out which was followed by one of the most lascivious licking and lappings I have ever experienced; for Bill Massey proved himself to be a shining exception to my opinion that unlike on the Continent, pussey eating is a neglected art in the United Kingdom and his wickedly clever tongue sent me off almost at once. When I felt my love channel spasm I scrunched my thighs tightly against the sides of his head as he gulped down my oozing love juice, smacking his lips noisily as he savoured its salty taste.

It was a real pleasure for me to repay the compliment so I settled Bill nicely on his back with his erect prick sticking up to attention as I knelt beside him and first thoroughly wet the mushroom-shaped dome of his helmet with my tongue. Then opening my mouth as wide as I could, I slipped the huge knob inside. His cock tasted quite delicious and I closed my lips around it as firmly as possible, working on the bulbous knob with my tongue as I eased my lips forward to take in every last inch of his gorgeous tool. I circled the base of his shaft with my hand and sucked lustily until his knob was almost touching the back of my throat.

Bill was now really excited and his hips lifted off the carpet as I increased the pace of my sucking. I cupped his hairy bollocks in my hands, feeling them harden as the sperm boiled up to shoot through his staff which jerked convulsively and then, whoosh! A veritable jet of juicy jism hit my throat and as even the most dextrous fellatrice will confirm, it is virtually impossible to swallow all a big-cocked boy's emission when your mouth is full of a shuddering shaft gushing a fast-flowing frothy hot spunk.

However, I swallowed as much as I could of his tangy flood until the fountain eased to a dribble though his shaft remained hard and stiff as I moved my mouth up and over his knob. Bill could see that I needed him inside me and he raised himself up and gently lowered his frame upon mine, one hand holding his wonderful cock which he laid carefully across my tingling cunt. He made a divinely slow and sensual entry, nudging his knob between my pouting pussey lips whilst I whispered fiercely, 'Go on then, Bill, fuck me with your big cock and make me spend,' as I raised my legs high to wrap them around his shoulders. His succulent tadger buried its throbbing length inside my cunt and his heavy balls couched themselves beneath my bottom. My cunney was delighting in this thrusting prick and each time he pistoned his prick forward my clitty stiffened, ever more eager, wanting more and more as he responded to my needs. His pumping quickened and my bum arched up as I received each glorious thrust; he grabbed my jouncy white bottom cheeks and we fucked away like a couple possessed, his thick prick sliding effortlessly backwards and forwards in my sopping pussey.

I tightened my cunney muscles as best I could

to feel the ridging of his knob and my cunt was now on fire as a raging orgasm swept through me. Moments later Bill's body went rigid and he shot his spunk with such intensity that my bush and thighs were lathered as his fervent cock spurted out its creamy tribute until he finally withdrew, letting his shaft rub itself amorously against my sticky cunney lips.

Our mouths came together in a more leisurely kiss as we rested our warm bodies in a sweet embrace, but then to my horror I noticed that we had spent so liberally that our mingled love juices had made two large damp patches on Kathie and Marcella's expensive Persian rug.

'Oh heavens, Bill, look what we've done!' I exclaimed, clapping my hand to my mouth. 'We've marked a valuable carpet and I know how difficult it is to clean off spunky stains.'

'Don't worry your pretty little head about it,' advised Bill, scrambling to his feet and hastily slipping on his drawers and trousers. 'Lock the door behind me after I've gone but listen out as I'll be back in a jiffy.'

He ran lightly to the door but returned only a few moments later carrying a small bottle of silvery liquid and a soft cloth. 'This will do the trick,' he said confidently. 'It's a bottle of Professor Mackswell's Theatrical Stains Remover, Jenny, which is widely used in the theatre for as you can imagine, costumes are dirtied from make-up, powder and goodness knows what else.

'Look, I'll dab some on to a clean cloth and you'll see the offending marks vanish like magic,' he added as he set to work.

Sure enough, Professor Mackswell's potion worked a treat and I was very relieved not so much that the evidence of our fucking had been removed but of course that no permanent damage had been done to our hostesses' carpet.

'There, I told you that Professor Mackswell's formula removes the most stubborn stains,' said Bill with satisfaction, 'and strangely enough John Clarke, a Varsity friend of mine who is now resident in Australia, tells me that he finds it an excellent fertiliser and his dahlias always win prizes since he began to treat them regularly with the Professor's elixir.'

'I don't believe you,' I chuckled as I started to slip into my clothes.

'It's true enough,' protested Bill. 'John became so attached to his flowers that his colleagues in Government House, Melbourne made up a little rhyme about him which goes:

> *There was a young chap in Australia*
> *Who painted his arse like a dahlia*
>   *Tuppence a smell*
>   *Was all very well*
> *But threepence a lick was a failure.'*

I smiled dutifully and I reflected how odd it is that of all poetic forms, the limerick is the only one which has steadfastly remained thoroughly lewd despite the vain attempts of Reverent Bowdler, Mr Lear and Mrs Nayland to wash away their vital vulgarity. As has been written:

> *Miss Limerick is furtive and mean;*

> *You must keep her in close quarantine,*
> *Or she sneaks to the slums*
> *And promptly becomes*
> *Disorderly, drunk and obscene.*

However, I digress, diary, though there is little more to report about the morning except what I had gleaned from overhearing Laura and Osbourne's conversation before breakfast; sure enough, when we rejoined the others, Kathie suggested that, after luncheon, we should drive into Chichester and spend the afternoon walking around the town: 'Would you mind very much if we borrowed your motor-car, Jenny, and Marcella will take our vehicle out for a spin?'

For some odd reason, it surprised me that the pretty young girl was capable of driving a motor-car and perhaps this showed in my face because a cheery grin broke out over Marcella's face and she said, 'Don't worry, I'm a good driver. The company owned by a close friend of my father built your car and Mr Royce himself taught me how to drive.'

'What, you've met Mr Henry Royce himself?' gasped Geoffrey Manning. 'I would love to meet him if only to shake his hand.

'I'm a motoring enthusiast and I'd give my right arm to drive one of his cars. Rolls-Royce cars are the finest in the world and your father's Silver Ghost, Jenny, is the best of them all [the name was taken from the silvery aluminium finish of the bodywork and remarkable silence of the engine – *Editor*]. I looked in for a time at the RAC Trial two years ago when a Silver Ghost completed a fifteen-thousand mile run.'

'Well, you are very welcome to drive my father's car this afternoon, Geoffrey,' I said with a little wink to the others, 'and there really isn't any need for you to amputate a limb to do so. Osbourne will be only too delighted to have some time off.'

These words made dear Geoffrey as happy as a sandboy and I knew that Osbourne would be similarly overjoyed as this would allow him to spend the afternoon fucking Laura, although I did not begrudge him his duty free hours. After all, although well paid (I believe his wage was as high as £130 per annum), he was on call at all hours and besides driving he had to wash the car after every journey, keep the interior spotlessly clean and be out in all weathers with no more shelter than a coachman of fifty years before. I have often wondered whether it is sheer snobbery that has made motor-car designers deliberately leave the poor driver out in the cold.

We marched into the dining-room for luncheon where we ate a splendid meal of home-made vegetable soup, mullet from the River Avon across the county, roast chicken and a dessert of fresh fruits. After this simple repast we sallied forth to the cars for our short journey into town. As I expected, Osbourne's face lit up when I told him that his services would not be required and Tony Hammond and Kathie joined Geoffrey and myself in the Rolls, leaving Bill Massey to accompany Marcella in the Wolseley which she and Kathie had purchased when the girls decided to live together.

Once we were ready to go, Geoffrey needed little instruction on how to drive and on the quiet road into Chichester, his only problem was to drive at a low enough speed for Marcella's vehicle to keep pace with us. 'Changing gear is almost a pleasure,' exclaimed Geoffrey as he slowed down to a halt to let a flock of sheep pass over the road. 'It's usually such a dreadful business that one can be jerked almost into the back seats, but on this car it's quite simple and anyhow you can drive from five to fifty without even having to change gear.'

He was patently sorry that our journey took so little time but we parked our cars near the cathedral and began our tour there. Much of the impressive building dates from the thirteenth century though the seventeenth-century tower built by Wren collapsed in 1861 during violent storms and it took six years to reconstruct the steeple. We admired the Saxon sculptures and the wall paintings and the wood carving and lovely stone tracery of the south window.

Then we strolled through to the eighteenth-century Council House in North Street which contained some excellent paintings and old furniture and who should we see just as we were crossing the road to make for Guildhall in Priory Park but Geraldine Flynn, a dear, close friend from my early schooldays in Devonshire with whom I regularly keep in touch by letter even though our paths do not actually cross more than three or four times a year. Geraldine, who I will now refer to as Gerry for she preferred to be known by this shortened form of her name (like

99

myself of course – I was only addressed as 'Jennifer' by my Mama or a tutor when I was being called to account for some naughtiness though woe betide anyone addressing me as 'Jen' which I dislike intensely).

Anyhow, Gerry was about to climb into a car the door of which was held open by a large Negro chauffeur and I called out to her excitedly, 'Gerry! Gerry Flynn! Hi there!'

She looked across the road to where I was frantically waving and her pretty face was wreathed in smiles when she recognised who was calling her and called back, 'Jenny, Jenny Everleigh! What a lovely surprise!'

I told my companions to wait for a moment and I walked across to Gerry and we exchanged a big, warm hug and kiss. 'What brings you to this part of the world?' I exclaimed because Gerry lives with her parents in King's Road, Chelsea although, as one would deduce from her patronym, she is of Irish extraction and her father owns huge tracts of land in County Donegal. However, Gerry is of a radical political persuasion and (much to her rather stuffy parents' displeasure) is an active member of Mrs Pankhurst's Women's Social and Political Union and a supporter of Irish Home Rule to boot. However, like Mrs Pankhurst's daughter Sylvia, she is a pacifist and abhors the use of violence to promote her views although she regularly takes part in peaceful demonstrations to promote her ideas.

I must also add that Gerry is a true beauty who has been blessed with a finely formed face with almost jet-black hair which falls down in ringlets on to her shoulders. Her skin is flawless and fresh and her eyes are of a divine blue and I noticed that though Gerry is now twenty-four, under her high-necked blouse, her bosoms were still as firm and thrusting as when she was sixteen and stealing her first kisses from my cousin Ronald at her birthday party.

'My parents have gone over to Ireland for three weeks and I'm staying for a few days with Gillian Glynde-Powell and her brother Edmund at their country cottage near Sidlesham on Selsey Bill,' she told me, and I must have raised an eyebrow because the Glynde-Powells were known to be members of Sir Lionel Trapes' ultra-fast South Hampstead set back home in London. Both brother and sister were artists and Gillian's Sussex landscapes were exhibited last year at Count Gewirtz's Allendale Gallery. Edmund, however, was in his own words 'a mere dauber' but had built a certain reputation as a critic, writing occasionally for *The Times* and *Country Matters*. He also enjoyed an even more substantial reputation as a first-class cocksman amongst the South Hampstead fraternity as did Gillie for her supposed predilection for the delights of Lesbos.

I explained how I came to be in Chichester and Gerry looked at my companions and said, 'Jenny, do my eyes deceive me but isn't that nice-looking fellow the brilliant young archaeologist Tony Hammond who is working in Spain with Sir Meyer Wantman?'

'Yes, that's right, do you know him?'

'Oh yes, we've met a couple of times before and I'd love to get to know him better. I studied under

Sir Meyer at a summer school he kindly headed for a couple of weeks when he came back to Britain for a short rest last year and it would be most interesting to find out what has been happening in Spain since then.'

She lowered her voice and whispered in my ear, 'I also hear that Tony's a very good fuck, Jenny. Would you know if there's any truth in this gossip?'

'You haven't changed, Gerry,' I chided her, much amused by her bluntness. 'Still, why shouldn't one call a spade a spade? Anyhow, the answer to your question is yes, he has a thick cock and knows how to use it.'

'But not as thick as Charlie's,' she muttered, jerking her head back to her chauffeur. 'Gillie brought him over from Barbados and he's *very* well endowed, I can tell you, though I've only been able to sample his goods a couple of times because Gillie keeps the poor man fully occupied, if you take my meaning.'

'Really? But I thought she was supposed to be a tribade,' I commented.

'Indeed she is and, as you know, I take pleasure in varying the menu occasionally with another girl, but she also enjoys a good stiff prick in her cunney as well. Look, why don't you all come back to Gillie's for tea? Edmund is up in London till tomorrow and we're all alone. She would be delighted to meet you and your friends.'

'Well, I can certainly ask them,' I said and we strolled across the road where I introduced Gerry to the group.

'We've met before,' said Tony Hammond

promptly, taking Gerry's gloved hand and pressing it to his lips. 'How very nice to see you again, Miss Flynn.'

'And to see you, Mr Hammond,' replied Gerry sweetly. 'I'd love to hear all about your adventures with Sir Meyer in Spain.'

And Gerry then repeated her suggestion that we joined her for tea; as by now my friends were a little tired after our walk, it was no surprise that they accepted her invitation and I noted how Geoffrey Manning in particular was delighted to take tea at Gillian Glynde-Powell's, doubtless because it meant a further spin in my car! So Gerry used the public telephone at the Council to call our hostess to ensure that all would be well and she came out saying that Gillian would be as pleased as Punch if we would come over especially as she had just received a telegram from Edmund to say that he would not now be returning from London until the day after tomorrow.

We stayed in Chichester a little longer and then drove in a three-car convoy to the Glynde-Powell house on Selsey Bill which is a very pleasant part of the county. The situation of the promontory is admirable for whilst it gets all the breezes that blow, it is sheltered from the roughest weather by the Isle of Wight. Nevertheless, in case the mild zephyr decided to increase in strength, Gillian had instructed her servants to lay tea in the drawing room. And what a tea had been laid on, a remarkable undertaking at such short notice! There were muffins, crumpets, scones, sandwiches and cake and we were soon all chatting away like old friends.

At our hostess's request, Geoffrey, Bill and Marcella joined her for a rubber or two of bridge whilst Gerry, Tony and I went for a walk in the garden. Gillian's gardener had slung a hammock between two trees and as I had the distinct feeling that my presence was *de trop* as far as Gerry was concerned, I took the opportunity of telling my companions that I was feeling a little sleepy. 'But please don't let me prevent you from carrying on,' I said to them. 'I'll have a little nap in this hammock, and you can meet me back here in half an hour or so.'

To be honest, I wasn't that tired but I guessed that Gerry, who is of a very determined disposition, had certain private plans for Tony Hammond which did not include my presence! However, I had no objections to being left behind even though it was well over an hour before the horny girl returned to the house with Tony, both of them looking slightly dishevelled and out of breath.

But there was a copy of *Harmsworth's Magazine* in the hammock and inside the magazine was a letter Gillie had received from a friend, Diana Cavendish, with whom I was acquainted when she lived in London. And here I must admit that I had no excuse except boredom, for I picked up the letter and began to read what turned out to be a rather steamy epistle from Diana who was married a couple of years ago to Lieutenant Kenneth Warringsford of the Fourth Yorkshire Cavalry Regiment.

Now there were murmurs in Society about the suitability of the match, for Diana was of a sensuous, passionate nature whilst her husband was hardly known for his prowess in matters of l'art de faire l'amour. Regretfully, I must also note here that in my experience, the pricks of military officers (as directly opposed to the privates and N.C.O.s which have much to commend them) rarely live up to expectations. They may strut and brag at their clubs or in the mess, but all too often they prove unable to match their boastful words with their deeds and cavalry officers in particular are perhaps the most disappointing of all. Perhaps the tightness of their uniforms has a bearing on the matter, although one would imagine that all that horse-riding would stimulate their bodies to give some great performances as far as their nuptial duties are concerned. After all, many county girls, who refuse to ride side-saddle, avow that there is nothing like a well-conditioned stallion moving between their thighs or a good gallop over rough country to set them up for a vigorous fucking in a haystack whilst the blood is still warm.

Alas, Diana's letter confirmed this general rule for although she was a keen horsewoman and looked forward to many happy fucks in the open countryside on the large Warringsford estate, her husband seemed to prefer hunting, shooting and fishing to spending any time in her company and the only way she could stiffen his cock was to pretend she was the head prefect at his old boarding-school and reprimand him for some infraction of school rules. Then she had to command Kenneth to take off his pyjamas and bend down and touch his toes before administering six strokes of the cane on his bare bottom.

Yet in case, dear diary, you think I am filling your pages with idle gossip, let me at least state that I have penned the above in mitigation of Diana's conduct which, as you will see from the contents of her letter to Gillie Glynde-Powell, is not what one would expect of a recently married young lady. The germane portion of this letter reads as follows:

Therefore, as you can well imagine, I was feeling very disgruntled on Tuesday morning when without so much as a by your leave, Kenneth suddenly announced that he was off the next day to Wiltshire for a fortnight's manoeuvres on Salisbury Plain with his Regiment.

He said he would be out all day on Army business and would not return home until six o'clock. After he left the house I decided to take my hunter out for a ride and I went upstairs and changed into my riding clothes. However, after I had pulled on my tight-fitting riding breeches, I was irritated to discover that my riding boots were not in the cupboard. I had left them in the stable to be cleaned but Tommy, the new stable boy, could not have yet brought them back to the house. As I walked down to the stables, I resolved to speak sharply to Tommy for though I had already noted with some relish his curly hair, delicately featured face and lithe muscular young body, he could not have been much more than sixteen years old which is why I was so shocked at what I was about to see.

The doors of the stables were unbolted and slightly ajar and at first I thought that I was alone. But then I thought I heard a scuffling sound coming from the loft and so I did not call out to announce my entrance but instead made my way quietly up the ladder to see whether I had been mistaken or whether indeed there was someone up there.

Gillie, I was far being mistaken! For in the loft, kissing and cuddling on a pile of straw were none other than Tommy the stable boy and Beattie Jardine, the seventeen-year-old daughter of the gentleman farmer whose estate bordered our own. Beattie must have brought her horse to our stables for she had discarded her jacket and was wearing only a snug-fitting white singlet and a pair of tight twill riding breeches. Tommy had shucked off his shirt and was wearing only his blue denim working trousers as they lay back in their bed of straw. Tommy's hands were caressing her rounded curves which hung like soft fruit and the little minx was not averse to pulling off her singlet and letting the boy toy with her naked young breasts. As she turned away for a moment to place her singlet over a wooden rail behind them, she leaned forward and through her open legs her pouched love lips could be seen straining through her skin-tight breeches.

Meanwhile Tommy busied himself with unbuckling his belt and pulling off his trousers and seeing what he was about, Beattie coolly followed suit and with a whispering noise she tugged down both her breeches and knickers until they were down at her ankles. Tommy stood up to assist her as she stepped out of them and I could see an enormous bulge in his undershorts.

'Lie down and I'll play with your cock, you naughty boy,' she said teasingly. 'No other girl can toss you off so nicely, can they?'

'Head to tail, Beattie!' gasped Tommy as she fished out his erect pink shaft from the slit of his drawers. 'Oh, please! Let's lie head to tail!'

'Ah!' whispered Beattie softly. 'You rascal! If we do that you will want me to suck your prick.'

He nodded his head and the girl laughed as she lay down on the straw. 'Come on, then, but you must lick me out first,' she said and Tommy leaped down with his head level with the tops of her thighs. He licked his lips and then bent his head downwards to kiss the curtain of silky brown hair which covered her pussey. I could hear his lips slurp along the slit as she grasped his stiff cock and slid her hand up and down the throbbing pole as she cried out, 'Yes! Yes! Run your tongue all along my crack – I love it! Now suck my cunney and make me spend!'

Tommy licked and lapped at her wet pussey until with a shudder she squealed as she achieved her spend, and then she turned her attention to palating his prick which she now clutched in both her hands.

Even though she was only sweet seventeen, Beattie showed herself to be a deft fellatrice who clearly needed no encouragement to suck Tommy's cock. She began by tonguing his shaft, licking and lapping in long, lingering strokes until she reached his bursting ruby helmet which she greeted with a series of hot, liquid kisses which pushed him to the very edge. Her wicked little tongue now circled his knob, savouring its spongy texture and he moaned in delicious agony as her teeth scraped the sensitive ridge of his knob. Carefully, she drew him in between her lips, sucking slowly as she took as much of his prick as she could in her mouth and then let her head bob up and down as she let go of his cock to let her hands snake downwards and frig her still sopping cunney.

No cock could take much of this treatment without disgorging its precious creamy cargo and Tommy panted, 'I'm coming, Beattie, I'm coming!' and she craned her neck forward and somehow managed to cram the entire length of his palpitating penis into her mouth, her lips almost touching his balls. With an anguished cry Tommy shot his load of jism into her mouth as he scaled the very highest peaks of pleasure. He pumped a copious emission of spunk between her lips and she greedily milked his twitching tool of sticky white sperm until he groaned and she opened her mouth to let go of his now shrunken shaft.

'There, wasn't that nice?' enquired the pretty girl and Tommy groaned, 'Oh yes, it was wonderful, Beattie, but when will you let me fuck you? Every night I think about nothing else and before I go to sleep I just have to toss myself off or I'd lie awake all night.'

'I've told you before, you'll have to wait,' she said, wagging a reproving finger at him. But then she smiled and added brightly, 'However, if you're a good boy, I might let you have me on your birthday next month. I don't suppose you'd want anything else as a present.'

My hands trembled as I put down the letter and I leaned back in the hammock. I reached down and stroked my own pussey which had begun to tingle and moisten as I read this uninhibited correspondence. It reminded me of a letter Lady Paula Platts-Lane had sent Sir Ronnie Dunn which the randy baronet had showed to me after we had just enjoyed a delicious post-prandial fuck at the Jim Jam Club [see Jenny Everleigh 10: Canadian Capers – Editor]. Poor Lady Paula had also married a man who, being of the homosexualist persuasion, had little inclination to perform his husbandly duties and Lady Paula's pussey was forced to rely on the thrillingly youthful tools of two good-looking stable-lads for company. Was Diana Warringsford also about to seek cuntal comfort from the willing prick of young Tommy?

I took a deep breath and read on.

'As the couple now began to get dressed, I quietly made my way down the wooden ladder and walked back to the door. I was feeling rather frustrated and rather wickedly I banged open the door and shouted, 'Hello there, is anyone here?'

There was a rustle from the loft and Tommy called down, 'I'll be down with you in just a minute, ma'am.'

Then down he came as bold as brass and I asked him rather coldly what had happened to my riding boots. His face flushed a deep red as he put his hand to his mouth and said apologetically, 'I'm dreadfully sorry ma'am, they're still here. I forgot to take them up to the house, but I have cleaned them and they look fine.'

Before I could say anything further, Beattie came down from the loft as bold as brass. 'Hello, Beattie,' I said with feigned surprise. 'What brings you to my stables?'

'Oh, I've been out for a ride and I came here to return a book that Papa borrowed from Lieutenant Warringsford. I was going up to the house but whilst Tommy was here I asked him to show me the old bridles you have in the loft as I have my twin cousins coming to stay with us this weekend and I was going to ask you if you had a bridle we could borrow for a few days.'

This was a good enough alibi and so I said, 'Well, I've saved you the journey, Beattie. Do you want to take them now?'

'No thank you, Mrs Warringsford,' she answered

sweetly. 'But may I leave the book I have to return with you?'

'Of course,' I said and she took it out of her saddle-bag and gave it to me. Then with a nice 'good-bye' she led her horse out of the stable and trotted away.

I did not mention a word about what I knew had been going on to Tommy but I knew from the moment I heard the hooves of Beattie's horse getting fainter and fainter that I had to fuck this beautiful boy. Finding a way to do so was the next task but a way soon suggested itself to me when Tommy went off to collect my boots. I sat down on one of the chairs placed along the wall specifically for riders wishing to change their footwear and when Tommy came back, I told him to kneel down and take off my shoes.

When the lad straddled the low bench at my feet and lightly grasped my calf to remove my shoe I could think only of his generously proportioned young prick and I became more aggressively brazen than I have ever been before in my entire life. For I so craved to feel his hard smooth shaft slewing in and out of my juicy cunt that after he had removed the other shoe, I made him hold my riding boot in which he thought I was going to put my foot. But I had another idea in mind . . .

'Stand up, Tommy,' I ordered and he did as I asked. Then I slowly raised my foot and ran my toes all the way up the front of his leg to his waist and then I moved my foot across and rubbed my toes against his cock and balls. The effect was electric! His jaw slackened and his mouth hung open as I said slyly, 'Has Beattie Jardine ever done this to you? It's nice, isn't it, being wanked by a girl's toes though I grant it isn't as nice as being sucked off and Beattie looks as though she knew what

111

she was doing just now when she gobbled your lovely big cock.'

He recoiled and stood trembling with his hands at his sides. 'Oh, don't fret, Tommy,' I continued impatiently. 'I won't be cross with you as long as you are still capable of carrying on the game you were playing with Beattie. Now let's go back up to the loft and see what you have to offer.'

The idea of fucking the mistress of Warringsford Hall obviously appealed to Tommy for he followed me up the ladder and as soon as we reached where he had had his fun and games with Beattie, I turned round and cupped my hand to his crotch and massaged a beautiful hard bulge there. I kissed him on the lips and Tommy rubbed my titties with one hand and fondled my bottom with the other.

I pushed him to his knees as I unbuckled the belt of my jodhpurs and unbuttoned the breeches before wriggling out of the tight-fitting trousers. I was wearing only socks which Tommy pulled off as I lifted first one foot and then the other and then I took hold of his hands and placing them on my waist, I told him to roll down my knickers. Again, he obeyed and I needed to give no further instructions because he then started to tongue my thighs, licking his way up to my pussey and the feel of his firm tongue lapping along my cunney lips was nothing short of exquisite. Then he began to lash at my clitty which had popped out of its hood and he licked wildly at my crack before plunging into my oozing cunt to tongue-fuck me.

I shivered as a spend surged through me and I gushed love juice into his mouth. He was pressing hard against my pussey lips and as his tongue twirled frantically inside my love channel I pulled his head even tighter *against me and I felt I would faint from the ecstatic waves of sheer pleasure which cascaded all over my body.*

'Now let's undress and you can fuck me with your cock,' I declared as I leaned forward and put my hands under his shoulders to raise him up from his knees.

In a trice we were thrashing around stark naked in the straw and Tommy was rubbing the swollen knob of his cock over my pouting pussey lips. He pressed forward and his gorgeous shaft slid into me. Despite his tender years, he felt so huge that I was afraid that I wouldn't be able to take it all but he pushed home gently until his balls were banging against my bum.

He pumped slowly, increasing the tempo gradually until he was fucking me with hard, deep thrusts which made his ballsack slap against my bottom as I wrapped my legs around him to pull his cock even deeper with each stroke and when he spunked it was like liquid fireworks exploding in my pussey.

However, I did not have the opportunity to read Diana Warringsford's epistle any further for at this juncture a housemaid came out into the garden and made her way to where I was lying. She asked me if I had seen a letter which her mistress had mislaid but which Miss Glynde-Powell believed she might have left in error with her magazine in the garden. Well, I could hardly dissemble to the servant and so I handed the sheets over to her without any hesitation, saying that I was just about to bring them inside the house myself.

Anyway, as aforesaid, Gerry and Tony came back from their perambulations looking somewhat worse for wear and I speculated that they had taken the opportunity to indulge themselves in what the lower classes colloquially call a 'knee-trembler' up against one of the majestic oak trees at the end of the garden. My speculation was soon to be justified because by the time we got back to the house the bridge party had ended and being a generous hostess, Gillian Glynde-Powell had opened a couple of bottles of champagne and we made pretty quick work of downing them. A maid brought in two more bottles and by the time we had polished these off, we were all slightly squiffy, which is no doubt why I cannot recall exactly how the size of Tony Hammond's erect penis became the subject of a heated discussion.

However, I most certainly do recall Gerry stating that she would not be at all surprised if Tony did not possess one of the biggest pricks she had ever been pleased to place in her pussey.

'But surely it cannot be as large as the appendage belonging to Mr Stuart Crichton of Glasgow,' said Gillian with some force. 'It is not for the size of his nose that he is known in Scottish society as the Cock of the North.'

'Yes, I believe I've seen a photograph of Mr Crichton's enormous equipment in the *Oyster*,' said Bill Massey thoughtfully, 'and I certainly couldn't match him for size.'

Kathie tossed her head and said, 'Oh Bill, it really doesn't matter a jot. Why do you men have such a fixation about the size of your pricks? I'm sure that you've all been told that it is quality and not quantity which is important although I must admit that Tony here has been blessed with one of the largest cocks in London.'

'Thank you very much,' said Tony modestly, 'although there is at least one gigantic prick in town which is much, much bigger than mine.'

'Really? And to whom does this noble instrument belong?' queried Marcella with interest.

'To Jumbo the elephant in Regent's Park Zoo!' answered Tony and this witty remark sent us all into peals of laughter.

We continued this light-hearted talk as we drank some more bubbly and then whilst Bill and Geoffrey excused themselves as they wished to play a game of snooker in the games room, Gerry Flynn insisted that whilst the other boys were out of the room, we girls looked for ourselves at Tony's tadger which even if not the biggest in Britain, she declared, was certainly a prime specimen which deserved to be viewed in all its naked glory. 'You don't mind, do you, Tony dear? You're not shy, are you?' she said and he gallantly replied that he had no objection at all to displaying his masculinity to the assembled company.

Tony stood up and Gerry sank down on her knees as she flipped open his fly buttons and drew out his thick tool in full erection. She lightly fingered the swollen shaft before grasping it firmly and asking Gillian, Kathie, Marcella and myself whether we shared her considered opinion that Tony Hammond possessed one of the most beautifully shaped cocks we had ever seen.

'Feel the velvety warm skin as smooth as polished ivory, Gillie,' Gerry urged our hostess.

'Oooh, I love the way the tool throbs when I rub my hand up and down it. And doesn't the curly crop of hair around the root nicely set off the magnificent pole and the hairy pouch underneath?'

'Let me see for myself,' said Gillian, also dropping to her knees and placing her hands around the thick shaft and planting a quick butterfly kiss upon the uncapped wide pink knob.

There was room for both girls to encircle their hands around the ample girth of this substantial love truncheon, and to the great delight of the owner of the palpitating penis, they soon replaced their soft hands by their tongues which darted out and licked and lapped at Tony's twitching tool. Now Kathie joined the fray, inserting her hand between the girls' faces to gently squeeze his ballsack whilst the girls' questing lips met at the moist mushroom head of his tremendous erection.

Tongue touched tongue as Gerry and Gillian jostled to suck upon their fleshy lollipop but this delicious sucking was too much for even the most sophisticated gentleman to bear and a stream of spunk burst from Tony's cock in a tidal rush of sperm, jetting jism into the girls' mouths, over their lips and into the air. Their hands stroked and traced patterns along the distended blue vein whilst Tony finished his spend in a juddering sexual ecstasy of relief.

'Now then, that's all very well, girls, but have you left something for Marcella, Jenny and myself to play with?' complained Kathie as she joined them on the carpet and, looking up at Tony

116

questioningly, she added, 'Can you raise your soldier into battle once again?'

'I think so – with a little help from my friends,' said Tony, taking her hand and placing it on his semi-limp tadger. She looked doubtful but his prognosis proved to be accurate because after a minute or two of sensual stroking and an occasional suck of his helmet, Kathie managed to prime his prick back up to a rock-hard state of erection.

Once she could see Tony's tool standing stiffly upwards, Kathie unbuttoned her skirt and pulled down her drawers before climbing upon his lap and lowering herself carefully but firmly upon his straining shaft. She began to hump herself up and down and rode the eager young man with style, maintaining a steady rhythm up and down on his rampant rod. As she breathlessly plunged down, he lifted his hips to meet her, and myself and the other spectators were treated to the tantalising sight of Kathie riding Tony's cock with enormous gusto, rubbing her swollen clitty button along the top of Tony's slippery, elongated member. She bucked harder and harder up and down on the glistening shaft and then cried out with sheer bliss as the great tremor of her climax swept through her body. Seconds later Tony gave a low growl as his prick disgorged a second copious emission of hot, frothy spunk inside Kathie's sensitive cunney.

The effect of watching this erotic exhibition naturally stimulated those of us who had a grandstand view of this prurient activity. Gerry had let her hand stray beneath my skirt and was rubbing it frenziedly across my pussey whilst we watched Kathie milk Tony's now exhausted cock.

'Let's go into my bedroom,' she murmured in my ear and I made only a token protest, saying that we might be missed by the others, but Gerry would have none of it as she pulled me up and guided me upstairs. In her bedroom I let myself lie on the bed and be undressed by the pretty girl. After she had pulled down my drawers and left me totally naked, Gerry then began to disrobe and when she stood framed in the sunlight, I thrilled to the sight of her beautiful breasts, ornamented with large, dark nipples, and her thick patch of crisp pussey hair through which I could see the pink cunney lips peeking out.

Gerry started to explore my own proud, rounded breasts which she cradled in her hands, teasing, squeezing and kissing and I closed my eyes, letting my head fall back on the soft pillow as I felt Gerry's lips close around my engorged nipple, sucking tenderly at first and then more hungrily and when her hand moved between my legs, I found her naughty stroking of my thighs extraordinarily arousing.

'Oooh! Oooh! You naughty girl!' I gurgled as Gerry slid her fingers into my fast-dampening cunney, moving them deliciously inside my cunt as the heel of her hand rubbed my clitty which was already as hard as a little acorn.

We pressed our slippery bodies together as we rolled from side to side and then Gerry moved her head downwards to my own blonde bush of wet, silky pussey hair and I trembled all over when she started to lick the sides of my long crack.

118

'Oh my!' I gasped when with a sudden dart, she plunged her pointed tongue in and out of my flaxen-haired mound in which she now buried her face. Her tongue revelled inside my love channel, flicking and sucking as one of her arms snaked round my waist and the other shot downwards to her own pussey where she frigged herself as she continued to lick and lap inside my juicy cunney.

'A-a-h-r-e!' I moaned as my body tensed towards a culmination of the tingling excitement which was building up between my legs and Gerry's tongue gave one final sweep of the sopping walls of my cunney and I began to spend, giving myself up to wave upon wave of erotic abandonment, panting and tossing my blonde head this way and that as the wonderful warmth of my orgasm flowed delightfully through my body.

Gerry gulped down all the salty love juice from my gushing pussey to the last dregs of my copious emission. Then she scrambled up to lie besides me and looking at me with her big, dark brown eyes she gave me a suggestive little wink and then closed her eyes, her large, snow-white breasts rising and falling, her tawny nipples still tantalisingly erect.

She turned to face me and we gracefully fell into each other's arms, cooing little endearments as we pressed our breasts together and rubbed our stiff nipples against the other's warm, receptive flesh.

I stroked her adorable titties with my fingertips and moistened my lips with my tongue before

119

lowering them to kiss each of her gorgeous nipples in turn, nibbling the taut, rosy flesh and sucking deeply, and Gerry purred like a contented kitten as my finger ran back and forth along the length of her juicy slit, lewdly massaging the tiny pink clitty. Then I parted her long legs and without ado moved my head across her tummy and kissed her black bush of pussey hair which was wet and fragrant with her musky love juice and I inhaled the perfume and probed with my tongue between her yielding cunney lips.

As I licked and sucked her aromatic cunt I felt Gerry shiver and tremble, her breath catching in little ragged gasps of pleasure as my tongue explored her depths. She had once told me that her most sensitive part was inside her cunt, about an inch from the entrance and I concentrated on that area with the tip of my tongue.

'Lovely! Lovely! Lovely! I'm going to come in your mouth, darling!' she panted, writhing delightfully as I pushed my mouth hard up against her cunney lips, moving my head back and forth as I sucked on her hard, swollen clitty, flicking my fluttering tongue in and out of her exquisite hairy quim, lapping up the cuntal juices; the squishy sounds of our love-making filled Gerry's bedroom so completely that it was with a shock that I felt a pair of strong male hands taking hold of my upraised hips and the insistent nudge of a throbbing tadger in the crevice between my bum cheeks.

If nothing else, instinct made me raise my bum and the owner of this proud prick now thrust further forward and sheathed itself fully in my tight cunney and he began pumping back and forth with a fine speed and no small amount of panting and moaning. But whose cock was slewing so sturdily in and out of my cunt in this wonderful doggie-style fuck? Tony Hammond was surely still being pleasured by Kathie and Gillian in the drawing-room so when I looked round, I was not surprised to see the lithe, athletic frame of Bill Massey behind me.

'Please forgive what many might call an unwanted intrusion, Jenny,' panted Bill apologetically, 'but I simply could not resist the sight of the sumptuous dimpled cheeks of your backside.'

'It's quite all right, Bill,' I gasped back as graciously as possible, for besides having Bill's sturdy stiffstander ploughing in and out of my cunt, I was still busy with Gerry's creaming cunney. 'We are well enough acquainted for you to fuck me in this way though I am sure you would agree that it would be *infra dig.* to slide your cock between the cheeks of a lady unknown to you.'

I wriggled my bum sinuously and worked my love channel up and down Bill's doughty shaft as he pounded faster and faster and his balls smacked a fine dance against the backs of my thighs until with a mighty groan he flooded my cunney with a torrent of frothy jism which sent spasms of sheer delight crackling through my veins.

As he withdrew his still twitching shaft from between my bum cheeks I now concentrated on

Gerry's delectable pussey. From the serrated red lips of her cunney, there now projected a stiff, fleshy clitty as big as my thumb. I opened my mouth and passed my tongue lasciviously about the sensitive love button, playfully nipping and biting it in our uninhibited love play.

'Oh! Oh! Oh! Here I go!' she wailed as she shuddered sensuously whilst I continued to flick my tongue against her clitty. She spent profusely over my face as I tongued her clitty to its ultimate excitement and Bill's physical prowess was such that he joined in the fun by presenting his glistening still stiff cock to Gerry who, nothing loath, licked and sucked thirstily on his thick shaft with evident pleasure whilst reaching across to delicately finger Bill's hairy ballsack.

He let out a low moan of delight and jerked his hips back and forth, fucking her mouth with great passion but also taking care not to choke the lovely girl with the splendid length and girth of his pulsating chopper. There seemed little problem for Gerry as she sucked in his cock to the very root and I could see that Bill was fast approaching a second spend. I could almost see the hot waves of spunk flood along his shaft as with a groan he flooded her throat with a copious emission of sticky white jism. Swallowing and sucking, she milked his cock so speedily that I giggled, 'Now then, Gerry darling, do remember what Nanny always told us. Every mouthful must be well chewed before it is swallowed.'

After Bill had recovered we dressed ourselves and trooped back to the drawing room where the others had also dressed although as we entered the room, Kathie was saying that it was a great pity that Tony Hammond could not manage a further cockstand as our kind hostess had only enjoyed the pleasure of a quick gobble of Tony's now crestfallen tool and Bill was sated whilst Geoffrey had excused himself as he needed to visit the bath-room.

'Please don't be concerned,' said Gillian with a smile. 'Don't forget, we have a fourth cock available in the house and I can always take my pleasure with Charlie.'

'Charlie?' said Marcella with a puzzled expression on her pretty face.

'My chauffeur,' explained Gerry lightly. 'Like many Negro men he is very well built and Charlie happens to have brains as well as brawn. He scraped together every penny he could to come to Britain from Barbados to complete his education and is currently studying at the London Hospital in Whitechapel. When he finishes his studies he plans to go home to Bridgetown and set up a hospital for poor people there.'

I was curious to know how Charles came to be in her service. 'So how did he come to work for you?' I asked and Gerry replied, 'Funnily enough, Jenny, this came about through the doing of a mutual friend of ours, Doctor David Lezaine [*see* Jenny Everleigh 4: The Secret Diaries *and* Jenny Everleigh 5: An American Dream for more about this raunchy medical gentleman – *Editor*], who is a patron of the London hospital.

'The hospital bursar approached David and asked if he knew of any employment for Charlie during the holidays as the small scholarship he won in Barbados barely covered his living expenses. So David kindly paid for Charlie to be taught how to drive and as I now have my own motor car, I said I would engage him for the summer.'

Tony cleared his throat and said, 'Well, that's a jolly decent thing to do, Gerry, but you mentioned that, er, Charlie, also performed other more special services for you.'

Gerry smiled lasciviously and said, 'Oh, that came about by pure accident. I went into his rooms above the motor-house to talk to him about a package of books I wished him to deliver to my Aunt Heather in Marylebone, but though I heard him singing, I did not realise that had just taken a bath. 'I won't be very long, Miss Geraldine, can you please wait for a couple of minutes?' he shouted out and I called back that I would indeed wait for him to finish his ablutions. Very naughtily, I put my eye to the keyhole and I caught sight of his superb nude body as he was towelling himself dry in his room.

'His physique was quite splendid – the muscles fairly rippled when he drew breath and expanded his magnificent chest and his torso narrowed down to a flat stomach and narrow hips and as he turned I caught sight of his heavy dangling cock which was of such a great thickness that I blinked and looked again to make sure that I was not mistaken. What an enormous shaft! My mouth watered just at the thought of seeing that huge prick standing up high in a full state – and even better if it were then lodged in my moistening pussey!

'Well, I waited till he came out of the bath with his bath-towel wrapped around his waist and as I sat on his bed and explained the nature of the errand I had in mind, my nipples began to tingle and erect themselves against the silk material of my chemise as I observed the handsome Barbadian. I am sure that Charlie must have had at least one British grandparent (many West Indians have European blood as the slavemasters were much taken by the beauty of the African girls brought over to the Americas in that vile trade in human cargo) for his skin was a light chocolate colour and his facial features were quite finely chiselled.

'When I had finished telling him about the journey I wanted him to make he said, "I'll go round to your Aunt's as soon as I've dressed, Miss Geraldine," but – well, I must confess that I was so taken with the handsome young man – as I stood up to leave, I gave way to temptation . . .

'Before Charlie could stop me, I unknotted the towel around his waist which fell to the floor and I now looked at his naked prick and balls. His cock was not fully erect but when I put out my hand and he felt my soft fingers roll back his foreskin to expose the gleaming rounded knob, his cock swelled up to its full majestic height.

' "Oh dear," Charlie gasped but I was more than happy to frig his immense throbbing tool and I instructed him to unbutton my dress as I kicked off my shoes.

' "Are you sure you know what you're doing?" he said hoarsely and I whispered that I was in full possession of my faculties and merely wanted a taste of his big, black cock.

'In a very short time I was as naked as Charlie and my nipples stabbed at his palm as he fondled each of my breasts in turn as we fell backwards on the bed. He knelt between my parted legs and I pulled his head to my bosoms and he kissed each hard red little tittie in turn whilst his arm reached down so that his hand was between my legs so that his fingers were free to play with the thick brush of curly dark hair which covers my pussey. He parted the rolled red lips of my cunney as I twisted and writhed with desire, rolling my belly silkily on his stiff black boner.

'As he continued to suck hard on my raised-up nipples, I threw back my head and moaned with joy as ever so tenderly, his fingertips traced the open, wet slit of my cunt, flicking lightly at the erect little clitty that was peeping out. I grasped hold of his huge pulsing pole and positioned his purple helmet between the dripping lips of my juicy pussey and I gasped with joy as he propelled in inch after inch until our pubic hairs were matted together. He pulled right back and then drove the full length of his powerful love trunk inside my cunney, again and again as I urged him on, closing my feet together at the small of his back to force even more of his thick prick inside me.

'It must have been some time since he had fucked, however, because very soon I felt Charlie's body stiffen and he withdrew his glistening cock and pumped creamy spurts of white spunk all over my belly.'

'Well, this fellow may have only been a humble chauffeur, but this was truly a gentlemanly way to behave for he had no idea as to whether your pussey was protected against unwanted sperm,' commented Marcella, and Gerry nodded her agreement, adding, 'Yes indeed, and because he could see that I had not spent, he insisted on licking me out. I lay back and relaxed whilst Charlie kissed my open cunt, running his tongue along the length of my parted cunney lips. I shuddered when the tip of his tongue found my hardened clitty and I began to jerk wildly from side to side as he gave it his best attention. His hands gripped my hips as I writhed around and he took his lips away from between my legs and started to rub and pinch my clitty with his thumb and forefinger.

'My hands flew to my breasts as I roughly massaged my nips as I heaved and humped until with a shriek I spent all over his fingers, clamping my thighs around his hand which remained tightly imprisoned between them until the delicious orgasm finally subsided.'

She paused and there was a moment's silence before Marcella sighed and said, 'Please don't think me impolite, dear Gerry, but I do wish you hadn't told us that exciting story in quite such graphic detail. It's made me feel extremely horny but I don't have time for any further fucking because we really must be on our way as we have a new guest, Mr Martin D'Elstree, dining with us tonight and we can hardly not be present when he arrives.'

As if on cue, Geoffrey came back from the bathroom and Kathie asked Glynda and Gerry if they cared to come back to Westhampnett with us for dinner. 'We will dine very simply,' she said frankly, 'but Marcella and I would be really delighted to continue this delightful party at our house.'

'Well, if you are sure it would be no trouble,' said Gillian doubtfully but after Marcella and Kathie assured her that for our wonderful cook, Mrs Hibbert, it was always a case of the more the merrier, Gillian and Gerry accepted the invitation, and so we left their house in cheery mood, looking forward to seeing the girls again later that evening.

Chapter 3

May 19th, 1909 (continued)

As soon as we arrived back at Westhampnett, we washed and changed for dinner and we were all sitting in the drawing room enjoying a pre-dinner drink when Martin D'Elstree arrived. I had met the gentleman before, for amongst his many artistic interests, he was the part owner with my old friend Sir Ronnie Dunn of the publishers Jackson and O'Connor. And it was on behalf of Sir Ronnie that I wrote my report on the British Book Trade [*see* Jenny Everleigh 8: Business As Usual – *Editor*] and how, of course, I came to befriend Kathie McGonagall.

But Martin D' Elstree's main interest was the theatre and he was an enthusiastic and generous member of the Stage Society which existed to give critics and enlightened members of Society at least a glimpse of plays the actor-managers and commercial managements either did not want or which were banned by the Lord Chamberlain's office.

After the necessary introductions had been made, I asked Martin if he had seen any good plays this season. 'There isn't much this year, Jenny,' he commented. 'Oh, I grant you there are some good musical shows, one or two sentimental comedies with a few good lines in them and there are plenty of the costume-and-rapier toshery for those that like that sort of nonsense. But there hasn't been anything one could get one's teeth into – and I don't think there will be much until we change this ridiculous censorship of the stage [censorship of the British theatre did not end until 1967 – *Editor*].

'For instance, Harley Granville-Barker has written a superb play called *Waste*. It's all about a politician whose career is ruined by a brief love affair and I suppose the combination of politics and sex was just too much for the Chief Examiner of Plays in the Lord Chamberlain's Office.'

'Yes, the yardstick Mr Redford [an ex-bank manager who had been appointed as the Examiner of Plays – *Editor*] uses to judge whether a work is suitable for public performance is quite ridiculous – there must be no discussion of religion, politics or sex! In other words, nothing about any of the three most important topics in the world!' he concluded with much feeling.

'Well, yes, I agree that Redford's censorship has been heavy-handed, but I would not categorise Granville-Barker's *The Madras House* as anything but a thundering good play which is also a clarion call for women's rights,' said Marcella as she handed Martin D'Elstree a large whisky and soda.

'Oh, I grant you that *The Madras House* is one of the few exceptions,' he agreed, 'but I would like to see more action against the pernicious idea that adults must be told what they can see or not see on the stage.'

Being a firm libertarian, I added my own two pennorth to the discussion and said, 'I couldn't agree more, Martin. It has always been the self-imposed duty of the upper classes to protect the lower orders from their own base instincts.'

There was little argument from the others and Gillian and Gerry now arrived to complete the party. We were called in to the dining room and I noticed with some amusement that Osbourne my chauffeur had been pressed into service as a wine waiter. He looked the part, being smartly dressed in a full butler's livery which I later found out came from the wardrobe of the amateur theatrical company to which Marcella and Kathie belonged. I raised my eyebrows as I passed by him but he murmured, 'Don't worry, Miss Jenny, I was a footman in Lord and Lady Hobart's before I learned to drive, so I'm not unfamiliar with this job.'

'I'm glad to hear it,' I replied as I took my place at the table. There was no problem in accommodating our extra guests and Mrs Hibbert, the cook, gave us a splendid meal of sole cooked in white wine, Riz de Veau aux Epinards, Saddle of Lamb, and then an Omelette Surprise, and the repast was concluded with a lovely vanilla ice cream, peaches, pears and oranges.

Osbourne performed his duties admirably and kept our glasses filled with chilled white wine and I was pleased to see that none of the ladies retired to leave the men to their own devices as the servants cleared the table and pots of coffee and *thé russe* were brought in. After all, why should women be treated like second-class citizens at the end of a dinner party?

I was very pleased that none of the men took up the offer of a cigar, although I threw a disapproving look to Gerry who lit up a cigarette for I cordially detest the smell of tobacco which lingers on the breath as well as polluting the air. However, we all partook of the excellent port and cognac offered by Osbourne who then very properly retired and left us to our own devices.

It was a warm evening and I asked if anyone wished to accompany me for a short walk outside. Kathie and Martin volunteered to join me and we strolled out into the grounds. Although it was now past ten o'clock, there was a full moon and consequently enough of what the Sussex yokel calls 'print moonlight' for us to follow the footpath.

We stopped and sat down on a garden bench and I asked Martin if he had performed on the stage lately, for amongst his other talents, he was a fine amateur actor who could have made a career on the professional stage if he had so wanted.

'I did have a small part in the Chelsea Players' production of Mr Jack Webster's new Scottish farce *The Man From Aberdeen*,' he admitted with a chuckle, 'and I do have a photograph of myself on stage with Miss Gillian Anthony but it is a somewhat unsuitable souvenir of the production.'

'Come, come, Martin, remember how we were talking about the undesirability of censorship?' I said teasingly. 'Do let Kathie and I see you dressed up in your kilt.'

He grinned and said: '*Touché*, Jenny,' as he dived

into his inside jacket pocket for his wallet. 'But before I show it to you, I should tell you that our mutual friend Colonel Gibson of Edinburgh assured me it was *de rigueur* that nothing should be worn under the kilt.'

'Quite so,' said Kathie solemnly although a smile began to play around her lips. 'Hence the old music hall joke of a girl asking Jock, "Is there anything worn under the kilt?" and he replies: "No, nothing's worn at all, Miss, everything there's in perfect working order." '

We laughed heartily and Martin sportingly took two photographs out of his wallet and showed them to us. 'I should explain that we were required to perform a vigorous Highland Fling and unfortunately the whirling motion caused my kilt to fly up and expose . . . ' his voice trailed off as Kathie pulled the photographs from his hand and she giggled, ' . . . your bare bottom! Oh well, what's the harm in that, Martin? Girls enjoy a glimpse of a man's firm bum cheeks, you know.'

'Maybe,' said Martin as he tried to grab back the second picture but Kathie was too quick for him and she held it away from him as she said, 'Ah, but this is even better, being taken from the front!' She passed the photograph to me and there indeed was Martin standing with his kilt being held up by two pretty girls and showing his Caledonian cock in all its splendour. His prick appeared to be very substantially proportioned and it did not escape me how his heavy balls hung low in their hairy sack.

'Two of the girls in the cast were rather frisky,'

explained Martin who was now blushing furiously although Kathie and I assured him that there was no need for him to be embarrassed. I said to him soothingly, 'You don't have to feel shy, Martin dear, both Kathie and I are more than familiar with the sight of a naked prick.'

'Yes, and I'd very much like to see the genuine article rather than a mere photograph,' said Kathie roguishly as she started to unbutton his fly.

'I say,' he gasped but made no move to prevent the randy girl slipping her hand inside his trousers and drawing out his erect shaft.

Kathie and I inspected his tool and we told Martin fairly and squarely that it was of a goodly size and well-fitted for all but the most cavernous cunt.

'I would be more than happy to entertain this cock,' said Kathie, moistening her lips voluptuously with her tongue.

Martin seemed taken aback so I chimed in, 'Good heavens, Martin, you seem astonished. Surely you recall your role as Bolloxonian in *The Sod's Opera* which you performed with distinction at the South Hampstead set's Christmas party two years ago. Why I can hear you declaim the lines now:

We may live without music, verses and art,
We may live without conscience and live without heart
We may live without friends, we may live without luck,
But life's bloody awful without a good fuck!'

'Button yourself up and come indoors and

Jenny and I will show you that we practise what she has just preached,' said Kathie, whose blood was up and who was more than ready to be threaded by Martin's magnificent member.

We walked briskly back to the house and as soon as we reached Kathie's room, our hostess was the first to strip off and Martin stared in wonder and then with unabashed lust at her exquisitely formed breasts, each crowned by a rosy red nipple set in a large rounded areola and without further words he stepped forward to take her into his arms as she pulled open his shirt. They sank down to the floor, exchanging the most ardent of kisses as the hot-blooded girl unbuttoned Martin's flies for the second time and released his straining shaft which sprang up like a flagpole between his thighs. She encircled his rigid rod with her hand and planted a wet kiss on the uncapped purple knob.

'A-a-h-r-e!' groaned Martin and he turned round to me and gasped, 'Jenny, please lock the door, somebody might walk in.'

'No one will come in,' I said cheerily as I helped pull off his shoes before beginning to slip out of my own clothes, 'and, anyhow, keeping the door unlocked adds an extra spice to fucking. Not that it would matter who might enter in this household – boy or girl they would simply ask if they could undress and join in!'

'Is that so?' he panted as Kathie now tugged down his drawers to leave him as stark naked as herself.

'Let's have some action rather than words, if you don't mind,' said Kathie, reaching out to pull his stiff prick towards her. Her pretty head plummeted down to Martin's groin. She wrapped her lips around the swollen helmet of his rigid shaft and her tongue fluttered out and circled his knob, and I could see her even white teeth scrape the tender flesh of his shaft as she sucked lustily away, drawing hard as though she were going to suck in all of his hot, blue-veined cock down to the very root.

Martin responded by jerking his hips to and fro as he fucked her mouth with great aplomb, and Kathie's tongue slithering round his tingling tool soon brought him to the brink of orgasm.

'I'm going to spunk, I can't stop!' he cried out through clenched teeth, his prick sliding in and out between her lips, and Kathie grasped his firm, manly bum cheeks, moving him backwards and forwards until with a final juddering throb he squirted his sticky tribute into her willing mouth.

She swallowed his copious emission joyfully, smacking her lips as Martin quivered with convulsions of delight. After she had milked his prick dry she lifted her head and said, 'M'mm, your jism is very creamy, Martin. It's one of the nicest I've ever tasted. Now let's get into bed and you can cram that big fat cock in my cunney.'

But instead of happily accepting this lewd invitation, he looked at her with a crestfallen look on his face and said sadly, 'There's nothing I would rather do, Kathie, but you gave me such a glorious sucking off that I'm afraid my John Thomas is temporarily out of service.'

'No matter, I'll come to the rescue,' I said and so the three of us climbed on to Kathie's bed. I rubbed Kathie's nipples against my palms as I rolled on top of her and the sweet girl smiled and said, 'Oh, Jenny, how delicious! Do you remember the first time we brought each other off in the back of Jonathan Claydon's bookshop in Falmer?' [*see* Jenny Everleigh 8: Business As Usual – *Editor*]

'Yes, it was absolutely divine,' I replied as Kathie spread her legs invitingly as I moved my head down to obtain a bird's eye view of her silky brown-haired pussey. My hands stroked her bare thighs and moved higher to her moist red cunney lips which were peeking through the furry moss and Kathie purred with sheer delight as I positioned my head between her thighs and buried my lips along her juicy crack.

My heartbeat quickened with erotic excitement as my tongue raked the erect button of her clitty before slipping down to probe inside her. Almost as if of their own volition, Kathie's legs splayed even wider, bent at the knees as she sought to open herself even more to my questing tongue. I slurped noisily on her pussey as I drew her cunney lips into my mouth, delighting in the clean, fresh taste as her hips thrust up in urgency, moaning and panting her pleasure as I lapped up the juices which were now flowing freely from her cunt.

I frantically attacked her twitching little clitty with the tip of my tongue and this set Kathie off on her final journey to the seventh heaven of delight. She jerked her hips upwards as the stiff, fleshy nut was drawn further and further between my lips and her hands grabbed my head, pressing my mouth even more tightly against her. Her legs folded across my shoulders as she screamed, 'Jenny, Jenny, here I go! I can't stop now! Aaah! Aaah! Aaah!'

The lewd girl spent profusely all over my mouth and chin as she swam in a veritable sea of lubricity, until she sank back exhausted by the joyous experience and I reached out and took hold of Martin's stiffening shaft and gave it an encouraging little rub. A few moments later we were engaged in a lascivious three-way kiss and I found myself on my back with Kathie lying on me, our breasts squashed together with her legs stretched out between mine. Martin was on top of her, trying to insert his cock between her bum cheeks but she turned her head round and said, 'Martin, would you mind if I rode a St George on your cock instead? I have a real fancy to do so. Jenny, I'll come back to your pussey, if I may.'

'By all means,' I said and moved myself across the bed to allow Kathie to twist round and frig Martin's cock with both her hands as he heaved himself round to lie next to me, his head on the pillow and his eyes closed in ecstasy as Kathie gently stroked the underside of his rock-hard cock.

'Is that nice?' cooed Kathie rhetorically as she allowed her fingertip to trace a path down Martin's shaft to underneath his hairy ballsack which made him shudder with gratification. After a while she closed her finger and thumb around the shaft, sliding them along its length and when she judged his bursting boner to be at its fullest extent, she climbed on top of him, with her knees on either side of his lithe, masculine trunk. The fiery girl then lifted her hips and crouched over his thick prick and rubbed her pussey lips across his straining round knob. Then she smiled knowingly as she took hold of his stiff cock and positioned his knob so that it was pressing directly on to her clitty; rotating her hips, she edged slightly forward, allowing his pulsating shaft to enter her. Ever so slowly she lifted and lowered her dripping cunt and each time more of Martin's member was crammed inside her until they melted away in sheer ecstasy with Kathie spitted on his rampant rod.

'Oh yes, that feels wonderful,' murmured Martin as he felt Kathie's cunney muscles contract and relax as she rocked up and down on his sturdy shaft, moving backwards and forwards whilst he cupped her jouncy, uptilted breasts, flicking the hard, stalky red nipples between his fingers and rubbing them against the palms of his hands.

Faster and faster she thrust down to meet his frenetic upward pushes and Kathie bounced, shook and ground her hips, leaning one way and then the other so that his cock was sliding in and falling out – though never completely!

Martin now lifted his head to suck furiously at Kathie's titties whilst the friction of her love channel reached new heights, and it was impossible for either of them to hold back any longer. His proud prick spurted jets of frothy sperm up her love channel as Kathie yelped with delight and seconds later her own spend sent electric waves crackling through her frame whilst his spunky white jism bathed her inner walls and her whole body glowed with lustful delight as she lifted herself from his glistening deflating shaft and rolled her body next to mine.

'You enjoyed that fuck, didn't you?' I said a mite crossly because I had not yet been fucked myself and Martin's cock was now firmly *hors de combat* after being milked for a second time by Kathie's clever cunney.

'Have no fear, Jenny, I haven't forgotten about you,' said Kathie and she turned her pretty face to mine and began kissing my cheeks very tenderly as she tweaked my hardening nipples with her fingertips and it crossed my mind how different the delicate touch of a girl's hands is from that of a man. A delicious warm tingle spread all over my body as she slipped her tongue inside my mouth and I met it with my own, stroking it softly against hers and then I licked around the outside of her mouth and tasted the sweet flavour of her light make-up.

I pressed my hands against the smooth flesh of her soft, beautifully proportioned breasts and I made her large red nipples stiffen as I sensuously caressed them, an action that was made even more exciting by Kathie rubbing her hand against my bushy blonde mound and I could feel a warm moistness starting to form inside my cunney.

Kathie purred like a sleek, pampered kitten, stretching out her long legs and arching her back as she silently urged me to explore the crisp black bush between her thighs and so I let my fingers stray to the neat though mossy dark triangle and a tingly thrill passed through my body as the inviting rich lips of Kathie's cunt opened magically under my probing fingertips. Her cunney was marvellously soft and wet and I was amazed at how easily my forefinger slid into her welcoming love channel and how smoothly I could work it in and out of her sopping crack.

Still frigging slowly into her, I started to kiss her pussey, slithering my lips gradually downwards until they were directly over her quim. I could taste the tangy juices and I could see the sticky dew on my fingers as I plunged, one, two and then three fingers in and out of her soaking slit.

My tongue was now busy nipping at Kathie's swollen clitty when dear Martin kindly took hold of me by my waist and gently heaved my body across the bed whilst I was gobbling Kathie's sweet cunney. He raised my legs as he propelled me a full one hundred and eighty degrees so that Kathie and I were now in a perfect *soixante neuf* with my cunney directly above her lips and my chin resting on her pussey hair as I continued to nip and suck her erect little love button.

I gasped as I felt Kathie's mouth flick across the damp grooves of my cunt and I forced my pussey against her mouth until she was comfortably sucking away at my cunney, whilst I kept my own tongue darting across her twitching clit. She spent in a little series of spasms that made her soft young body writhe beneath me but she did not neglect my needs even at the climax of her own orgasm and all the while her lips continued to suck greedily on my cunt, her tongue lapping non-stop inside my dripping crack until I too was brought shuddering to new, previously unscaled

141

peaks of pleasure as I rubbed myself off against her mouth.

Perhaps it was the creaking of the bed allied to our cries of ecstasy as we revelled in our erotic entertainment that alerted other guests in the house as to what was taking place in Kathie's bedroom, but as Kathie and myself lay exhausted with our hands around Martin's cock, frigging his stiffening shaft up to a further erection, I could see the shadowy figure of Tony Hammond in the background, undressing as quickly as he could. Meanwhile, Martin moved his head towards my face and kissed me, our tongues wiggling inside each other's mouths as Kathie began to open my pussey lips with her fingers. He then climbed on top of us and placed his knob against my mouth and I opened my lips and sucked in the smooth, mushroomed helmet, lashing the succulent shaft with my tongue before taking in another three inches of his delicious cock in my mouth.

Kathie now started to kiss my erect tawny titties and Tony Hammond now padded across to join us, his stiff, upright love truncheon in his hand and he slid in besides Kathie who grasped hold of his pulsating prick and guided his knob towards the lips of my cunney which opened like magic to enclasp the crown of Tony's huge cock.

All three of them were now fucking me, with Kathie licking my titties whilst she was frigging her own pussey, Martin's member plunging in and out of my mouth and Tony's tool slewing in and out of my juicy cunt. It was a gloriously exciting sensation and I came simultaneously both with Tony who spurted a tremendous torrent of hot seed splashing against the walls of my cunney, and Martin who filled my mouth with his frothy white spunk so well that I could not gulp it all down and some of the love juice dribbled down on to my chin.

This lascivious fuck so stimulated the boys that after Kathie and I rubbed their sticky wet cocks they were both able to continue pleasuring us. But this time we decided to pair off and I chose to exchange a passionate kiss with Martin for I had yet to experience the pleasure of his thick prick in my love channel. We embraced in a kiss of blazing ardour and then without further preliminaries his tongue moved downwards to circle one of my erect nipples and then the other as they hardened under his tongue. 'M'mm, there seems to be plenty of ammunition left in the arsenal' I purred as I ran my fingers down the length of his shaft and then delved underneath to caress his unusually heavy balls.

He smiled and slid his arm around my waist and pulled my bum up so that my pouting pussey lips were brushing against the tip of his knob. For a few moments he teased my tingling crack by rubbing his cock all along the length of my gash but then at long last he slid the bulbous helmet into my welcoming cunt and began fucking me with long, powerful thrusts.

I could feel his lovely shaft swelling up even more inside my cunney and he moaned with delight as he tweaked my titties with one hand and fondled my clitty with the other. My juices were now simply seeping out of me as he flicked my love button to and fro whilst he slicked his meaty shaft in and out of my sated cunney. His hips jerked backwards and forwards as he thrust his throbbing tool further and further inside me, reaming out the furthest recesses of my cunt and the walls of my cunney were opening and closing around his wonderful cock. And then with a hoarse cry he shot his load and creamed my cunney with a copious ejaculation of warm, glutinous spunk.

Now I reckoned that he would need some time to recover from his labours but I was wrong! As he removed his sticky shaft from my cunt I saw that it was still semi-erect and would need only a little help to regain a full stiffness. So I raised myself up and crouched down to clamp my lips round his gleaming knob and I licked up and swallowed the residue of our combined juices which were quite delicious. I lustily sucked on Martin's big balls before taking his wet shaft back into my mouth but though I tongued it up to its former majestic height and hardness, he quickly spunked a second time into my mouth and I swallowed the remainder of his frothy emission as his prick quickly softened to a drained limpness between my lips.

Whilst we had been engaged in this passionate copulation, Kathie had busied herself in sucking Tony Hammond's tremendous tadger. Martin and I looked on with interest as she ran the tip of her tongue around the edges of the springy cap of Tony's cock whilst she simultaneously squeezed his balls gently through their hairy bag of soft, wrinkly skin.

'Ooooh! Ooooh!' groaned Tony as he clutched

at Kathie's hair whilst she drew her warm, wet tongue right up the length of his swollen shaft. She pulled his rock-hard prick from between her lips and lapped up the pre-spend jism which had oozed out of the 'eye' on his knob and flicked her tongue delicately around his helmet before opening her mouth wide and sucking in his entire cock right down to the root. She sucked lustily as she bobbed her head up and down on his rigid rod and every so often she took her lips away from his glistening shaft to give his knob a swirling lick before plunging the pulsating pole back inside her mouth.

Now she rolled his stiff white column between the palms of her hands as she reluctantly withdrew her lips from this fleshy fat sausage for she did not want Tony to spend inside her mouth. So she scrambled round on all fours and thrust her firm young buttocks in his face, turning her head round to say lewdly, 'Come on now, Tony, I'd love a firm pressing of cock juice up my arse. But first smear your cock with the cold cream in the pot on the bedside table.'

This command was obviously music to his ears for he growled his thanks as I reached over to the bedside table and opened the jar concerned and plastered his prick with a liberal coating of cold cream. Tony then mounted her, his left hand prising open a channel between the cheeks of her splendid bum, and his right holding his massive blue-veined prick which stood mouth-wateringly rigid from its nest of dark, curly hair. He placed his knob carefully in the crevice between her buttocks and slowly forced his cock through her wrinkled little rear dimple. Kathie cried out at first but then her sphincter muscle gradually relaxed as his cream-coated cock entered the tightened orifice and she told him to sink his shaft in up to the hilt.

Tony leaned forward to slide his hands round her sides to fondle her breasts as he pounded in and out of the tiny, puckered rosette and Martin and I saw his prick slide in and out of its narrow sheath, plunging in and out of the now widened rim, pumping and sucking like the thrust of a steam engine.

'A-h-r-e! A-h-r-e! Go on Tony, fuck my bum, you big-cocked boy!' Kathie cried out lewdly as she reached back to spread her cheeks even further, wriggling her delicious backside from side to side.

'Oooh, Kathie, this is pure heaven, what a lovely bottom fuck! What warmth, what tightness!' panted Tony, patting her flanks and savouring the way the plump *rondeurs* of her gorgeous bum smacked against his belly and the sensuous movement of Kathie's hips sufficed to show us the pleasure she was evidently sustaining. He continued to pound away until Kathie let out a high-pitched yelp which Tony echoed with a fierce grunt as he shot a jet of jism inside her and they spent together in perfect accord. Then he withdrew his prick with an audible little plop and the four of us lay together in a sweaty tangle of arms and legs.

Martin and Tony were well on their way to the Land of Nod and this situation, which often occurs after a good bout of fucking well illustrates my contention that whoever coined the old saw about women being the weaker sex was a complete fool.

Oh, I grant you, diary, that men may possess more brute strength than women, but when it comes to stamina and a sensual appetite, the male animal simply cannot compete with the female of the species. Kathie and I were ready and willing to continue this erotic entertainment but despite all our efforts, Martin and Tony could not raise a cockstand between the pair of them. Perhaps we should not have been surprised for the penis is a contrary-minded little fellow, often whimsically disobedient to the desires of its master. Even the most generously endowed young man can find himself cursed with an unwanted erection whilst at the luncheon table or making a small purchase in a shop – though to add insult to injury, he can then find that when he has achieved his goal and bedded a willing girl, on the very eve of battle, his weapon remains stubbornly flaccid.

This affliction is one that affects all men, I thought to myself as I licked and sucked Martin D'Elstree's soft prick in an effort to transform it into a pulsating stiff pole which would stab squelchily in and out of my wet, yearning pussey.

But it was obvious that neither Kathie nor I would be able to raise any further interest from either Martin or Tony's cocks, so when there was a knock on the door, I hoped that it would be either Bill or Geoffrey in the hallway – who would come in and bring a fresh throbbing stiffstander to liven up the proceedings again.

Alas, although it was indeed Geoffrey Manning

at the door, from his dishevelled state, I could see that he had been copulating with one or more of the other three girls and that he also looked quite exhausted.

'I don't suppose you are up to fucking Kathie and myself?' I enquired and he replied with a rueful tone in his voice, 'Jenny, the spirit is more than willing but the flesh is equally as weak. I fucked Gillian twice and Gerry has just finished sucking me off and I don't think my poor prick will be up to the mark till the morning. Truthfully, I only came here to wish you all good night.'

'Well how about Bill?' asked Kathie but Geoffrey shook his head. 'Gerry sucked him off whilst I was fucking Gillian and she gobbled him whilst she finger-fucked Gerry and I was taking a breather. Your maid Laura just came in to his bedroom where we were engaged in our whoresome foursome and I think Bill's having her just at the moment as the other girls have now gone downstairs.'

'Is he now?' exclaimed Kathie, jumping out of bed. 'Well, I think that our guests' needs must be satisfied before those of the servants! Good night, Geoffrey, we'll see you in the morning. Jenny, you come with me!'

Stark naked, we walked across the landing and opened the unlocked door of Bill's bedroom and feasted our eyes on a fine erotic tableau. Bill Massey was lying flat on his back, completely nude, with his huge stiff chopper standing up as rigid as a flagstaff and young Laura, who only that very morning I had seen engaged in an ardent, impassioned fuck with Osbourne, my chauffeur, was rubbing his twitching tool with both her hands, frigging him up to bursting point. She was dressed, or rather half dressed in her black and white maid's uniform, for Bill had undone her top buttons and her creamy uptilted breasts had freed themselves of any covering and stood out proudly, naked and unashamed, mouthwateringly ripe for the touch of lips or fingers and indeed Bill reached out with both his arms and fondled her engorged raspberry nipples with his fingers.

Kathie looked on with mounting concern as Laura's soft fingers seemed on the point of bringing Bill to a climax. 'What are you doing with Mr Massey's cock, Laura? For heaven's sake, don't let him spend from a mere tossing-off – you should know better than to do that!' she said warmly, wagging her finger in disapproval at her servant.

'Sorry, Miss Kathie,' said the maid apologetically. 'I didn't think he was ready to spunk for a bit.'

'Well he was, weren't you, Bill?' declared Kathie as Laura adjusted her clothing and with a sulky pout began to button up her dress. Kathie sighed and added, 'Oh, there's no need for you to leave, Laura, although I thought you told me how much you wanted to fuck Miss Glynde-Powell's driver tonight if only to see whether it was true what you had heard about black pricks.'

'I know I did, Miss Kathie, but I'm afraid that Miss Marcella got there before me and she's in bed with Charlie right now,' replied Laura with some spirit, 'so I didn't think you'd mind if Mr Bill

149

fucked me because you've always said that I could have any of the gentlemen I fancied if they weren't otherwise engaged.'

Bill cleared his throat and now entered the conversation. 'Please don't be cross with Laura, I invited her up here myself,' he said to Kathie. 'I hope that I haven't broken the rules of the house by doing so.'

Kathie replied, 'No, not at all, Bill. As Laura has correctly pointed out, she is entitled to be fucked by any guest so long as the prick concerned is not wanted elsewhere.

'And just now I rather do fancy your nice cock,' she added, climbing up on the bed and wrapping her long fingers around his thick shaft which had drooped slightly since Laura stopped frigging it. 'I do like rubbing it and feeling it buck and throb in my hand.'

She sat down next to Bill who eased his hand between her unprotesting legs and ruffled the crisp dark hairs of her moistening muff. As Kathie continued to frig his big, stiff prick, he gradually opened the yielding lips of her cunney and began to finger-fuck her and he cried out, 'Faster, Kathie, faster!' as she worked her hand up and down his pulsating pole until the frothy white seed spurted out from the top of the purple domed head like a miniature fountain.

With his fingers still entwined in her hairy thatch, she moved over and knelt beside him to kiss and wash her tongue all over the sticky knob of his still almost fully erect shaft. He groaned as she tickled his hairy balls and licked all around his helmet and this made his prick swell up to its former rock hard stiffness. Then she swung her body across him so that the firm fleshy cheeks of her backside were pressing against his flushed face and when she sat down to fully straddle him, his lips were touching the sides of her dripping slit.

The sight of this lusty *soixante neuf* made my own pussey tingle and when Laura slid her hand around my waist, I responded by kissing the sweet young girl passionately on the lips and I laid her down next to Bill and Kathie on the bed. Then I draped her long legs over my shoulders and dived down headfirst into the curly brown tufts of her pussey which was already wet as I lovingly began to lick and lap around her juicy crack, forcing my tongue deep inside the warm, wet slit, sliding up and down the wide gash as I savoured the pungent aroma of the love juice which was already trickling out of her cunney. She squealed joyfully as I probed between her cunney lips and thrust my tongue roughly between them, chewing her clitty which I rolled and sucked between my lips as she writhed around, rubbing herself off against my mouth.

As I let the tip of my tongue dart in and out of her sopping snatch she grabbed my head and pressed my face firmly into her pussey as she wrapped her thighs around my head, and began to twist and writhe as the first shivery stirrings of an approaching spend began to spread from out of her cunt. Her love juice dribbled out from her parted love lips and her erect clitty swelled even more as I flicked at it gently with the tip of my tongue. I decided to move my hand up to my face and Laura opened her thighs for me to frig her slippery little clitty with my thumb.

Her yelps of joy were now joined by cries from Kathie and Bill who were finishing each other off in style next to us and after they had climaxed they watched Laura's body jerk wildly up and down as my face rubbed against her tufty bush. 'Yes, Yes, Yes!' she yelled as I worked my tongue in and around her cunney until my jaw was fairly aching.

But I was rewarded by the lovely young girl achieving a tremendous orgasm, splashing my mouth and nose with a flood of love juice as her cunney spurted its salty tribute which I gulped down until it finally subsided and we lay panting with exhaustion with my head resting on her sated crotch.

Although Laura may have only been a lowly housemaid, Bill insisted that being the only gentleman present, he would be the one to slip on a dressing gown and bring up a bottle of champagne from the ice-box. He returned in less than five minutes with two bottles of '04 Moet and Chandon, four glasses and a small bowl of fruit on a tray and (I should have noted earlier that thankfully Kathie had given him a room with a double bed) the four of us managed to squash in under the covers and enjoyed this much needed refreshment.

'How old are you, Laura?' asked Bill suddenly and the young girl blushed and replied, 'I'm eighteen, sir. Why do you ask?'

'Oh, no particular reason,' said Bill lightly. 'Only I've been asked by Jackson and O'Connor to help Dr Nigel Andrews prepare some extra material for the new edition of *Fucking For Beginners* which they will publish next year, and I would be most interested to listen to how a young girl like you, for example, crossed the Rubicon to womanhood. Your story might be very instructive for young girls in service and if we used it in the book Mr Jackson would send you three guineas [three pounds, fifteen pence in today's currency though worth considerably more in 1909, for, at best, a servant like Laura would only earn about thirty pounds a year plus her keep – *Editor*] for your trouble and of course we wouldn't use your name or give any details which might identify you.'

'I don't mind talking about my first threading at all,' said Laura, her large brown eyes shining brightly as she thought about what she could do with such an easily earned large sum of money. 'It happened here just a few days before my seventeenth birthday. I should explain that my family home is in Little Grafton, a tiny village some thirteen miles north east of Chichester. My father's head carpenter at Colonel Kitson's country house and my mother also works as a seamstress at Kitson Hall and I was expected to follow my two sisters who are also in service there. But I wanted to see more of the country and so I took up service with Miss Kathie and Miss Marcella. I'd only planned to stay for a year before applying for a position in London but I've enjoyed working here so much that I've never thought of leaving!'

'I suppose you attracted some followers when

you arrived here,' I commented and Laura nodded her pretty head. 'Oh yes, Miss Jenny, the boys flocked round after I arrived here,' she said innocently, displaying none of the false modesty which can be as foolish as overbearing pride,' and I was quite taken by the grocer's son, Jimmy Pickard, who delivers our weekly order from his father's shop in Westhampnett, and I was very pleased when he asked me to go to the Fair with him on the Easter Holiday.

'Now I should say here that I wasn't exactly ignorant about the birds and the bees – no country girls are! But back home I'd never gone much further than French kissing and letting a boy touch my breasts though once I let Patrick Janson pull my hand down and feel the hard bulge between his legs when we went for a walk in the woods and spooned on the banks of the stream which ran through the forest.

'Well, Jimmy Pickard, who was only three weeks older than me, by the way, had far more experience with girls than I had with boys and he urged me along the road of passion very quickly. We were soon cuddling passionately after we'd started walking out together. I'd let Jimmy cup my breasts with his hands but I'd never let him unbutton my blouse though I did feel tingly all over when I felt his stiff cock pressing against my belly when we kissed.

'Anyhow, he asked me to come with him to the Easter Fair on the coming Spring Holiday and Miss Kathie and Miss Marcella kindly allowed me to go with him for the day. We enjoyed ourselves very much at the Fair and Jimmy had brought us a packed lunch and we had a mid-afternoon picnic of sandwiches and beer on a quiet grassy knoll a half mile or so away from the Fair.

'I was wearing a frilly white blouse and as the weather was lovely and warm I had opened the top two buttons. I could see Jimmy staring at the firm swell of my breasts and I knew he desperately wanted to run his hands across them. Truth to tell, I decided that I would rather like him to do so and I snuggled up to him and turned up my face to his and kissed him full on the lips.

'A rush of excitement surged through me as he responded and our tongues forced their way between each other's lips and lapped against each other in the most voluptuous manner. As I had expected, Jimmy's hand slid up from my waist and I felt his hands close over my breasts. Then he undid the remaining buttons and slid his hand inside and pulled down the straps of my chemise and I lifted my arms to free myself of it in order that he could pull down the garment and free my breasts of all covering. When he saw my naked bosoms, Jimmy nearly choked with excitement and with one hand he squeezed my titties and he pulled up my skirt with the other.'

Laura paused for a moment to finish her glass of champagne and continued, 'Everything was happening so fast but it didn't occur to me to resist him. I just sat there soaking up the exquisite sensations of his kiss and the touch of his hands.

'I made no move to prevent his fingers reaching the top of my legs and he began to press his palm lightly on my pussey. Then he began rubbing it in an increasingly fast rhythm which had my whole body pulsing with pleasure and feeling so incredibly aroused that from then on I was putty in his hands and was glad and willing to let him do anything he wanted with me.

'I could feel him tugging down my drawers and automatically I raised my bum up to assist him in pulling them down to my ankles. Then he slid his fingers up and down my crack which was now quite wet and he slipped in two fingers between my love lips as he leaned forward and took one of my big, stiff nipples in his mouth and sucked it firm and deep into his mouth.

'Without any persuasion I reached out and fondled the rock-hard bulge which had formed in Jimmy's lap and which threatened to tear the grey cloth of his trousers. As if in a dream, I unbuttoned them and out sprang his huge prick, the first time I had seen a naked cock and I grasped the hot, throbbing shaft, gingerly at first, and then gently stroked it up and down, capping and uncapping the fiery red knob.

'Matters then took their natural turn and we both removed all our remaining clothes. I lay down on Jimmy's coat with his soft picnic bag as a pillow. Now Jimmy might have been just seventeen but he was no virgin and he was in no wild hurry to fuck me. He began this important stage in our love-making by parting my legs and kissing my very wet pussey. I love having my pussey kissed but he was the first boy to do so though one of the girls had brought me off this way after the Christmas party during my last term at the village school.

'Anyway, Jimmy let go of my breasts and moved

156

himself round so that his head was over my tummy and he licked and lapped at my cunney lips and then, oh my, I'll never forget how the tip of his tongue found my clitty and I twisted my thighs around his head as he sucked the love juice which was fairly dripping down the inside of my thighs as I spent in a quick little series of delightful spasms. We both knew that the time had come as he wriggled free and panting with excitement, he looked up at me.

'I want to fuck you,' he said hoarsely and I replied, 'Yes, I know and I want you to, Jimmy, but be careful and don't shoot your spunk inside me.'

'I won't,' he promised and he raised himself above my trembling body. I clutched at his gorgeous thick prick and eased the smooth knob between the pouting red lips of my cunney. Although I was technically a virgin, I had been diddling myself for some time and my hymen had long since been broken. My cunt was so juicy that I had little need to guide him for he entered me easily and for the very first time I gloried in the feel of a throbbing stiffstander inside my cunt.

'Jimmy was a very considerate boy and he slipped in his knob an inch or so and then rested. This gave me time to feel its presence and as he moved forward slowly I had time to feel how wonderful it felt to have this hot, hard fleshy pole inside me and how well suited my cunney was to hold and keep it there.

' "I'm not hurting you, am I?" he asked anxiously and I kissed him and told him how much I enjoyed the sensation of his lovely cock sliding in and out of my sopping love channel.

' "Push in harder and deeper," I urged him and he eagerly complied, moving in slow, rhythmic thrusts and I thrilled for the very first time to the wonderful waves of sheer ecstasy that spread out from my pussey as I felt his cock push in and withdraw, push in and withdraw, and how exciting was the squelchy sound as my juices eased the passage of his shaft. My sheath was now so well lubricated that we enjoyed a gorgeous fierce bout of fucking and every nerve in my body thrilled with rapture as I heaved my bum up to meet the pistoning strokes of his prick, winding my legs about him so that his large, hairy balls banged against my bottom as he buried his shaft in me to the very hilt.

' "I'm going to spunk!" he panted suddenly and to my frustration (although the lovely boy was right to do so for as I told you I had told Jimmy not to spend inside me) he pulled out his twitching tool which spurted out a fountain of frothy white seed all over my quivering belly. I rolled my fingertip in the sticky pool and licked it to taste the pleasant, slightly salty flavour of his sperm and Jimmy collapsed on me with a heartfelt sigh.

'Then he rolled over to lie next to me but my blood was up and I could see that his marvellous penis still looked heavy and capable of a repeat performance. So I told Jimmy to position himself on his knees in front of me and I opened my legs wide so he could see my pouting pussey lips for himself. Then I boldly took his hand and placed it full on my soaking hairy bush which I could see excited him for immediately his fingers splayed

158

my love lips and he ran the fingers of his other hand right down the length of my tingling crack.

' "Push your finger inside," I implored and when he did so, my hips rose to meet it. But what I wanted more than anything else was another bout with his majestic young cock! So I told him to sit back on his haunches and I wrapped my fist around the slippery wet length of his shaft, finding to my delight that it began to swell almost straightaway as I started to frig it and I could not resist jamming down his foreskin and delicately fingering the red mushroom helmet.

'But I knew that if I frigged him much more Jimmy would soon spend again so I lay back and he scrambled back on top of me again. I gave his hot cock a final squeeze before he slid his knob between my yielding cunney lips and I slipped my hands down his back to clasp the cheeks of his bottom to make sure he pushed in every last inch of his prick.

'Oh, what a wonderful fuck this was! My pussey throbbed and throbbed as his thick tool slicked in and out and I wanted Jimmy to spend inside me. It crossed my mind that my monthlies were only two or three days away, the chances of my getting into trouble were very small so I murmured in his ear that he could ride bareback this second time.

'That's all he needed to hear! Within seconds we were screaming together as we felt ourselves spending and the feel of his frothy sperm spurting inside my saturated cunney made me shiver with delight as my own love juice came flowing out of my cunt, mingling deliciously with his sticky jism that was creaming my cunt so beautifully.

' "Go on, Jimmy, fuck away!" I whispered fiercely in his ear and the darling boy obliged as with short, stabbing strokes he shot stream after stream of hot, juicy jism deep into my willing body. Then my own spend made me shudder all over as I also climbed the heights.

'We fucked quite a lot until Jimmy was sent to an agricultural college in Dorset last year though we do write to each other from time to time.'

There was a brief silence as Bill, Kathie and I digested this wonderfully told tale and Bill congratulated Laura on the truly excellent way she told her exciting story.

'Could you write down what you have just told us in the same, uninhibited style?' he asked her and she said she would like nothing better than to do so. 'I always enjoyed writing essays at school,' she said. 'Miss Arnold, our English mistress at school, said I had a natural talent and she always encouraged me to use my imagination and write stories. She told me that despite my lowly station in life, when I was a few years older I really should try my hand at writing a novel.'

'I agree with Miss Arnold, and you must send a script about your first fuck to me at Jackson and O'Connor's office. Miss Kathie here has the address,' said Bill, turning to our hostess with a chuckle and adding, 'I'm sorry, Kathie, but I think Laura might possibly be able to write a very interesting book and you may well lose a valuable servant but being a bookseller yourself, I know you wouldn't want to stand in her way.'

'Of course not,' said Kathie, 'though you'd better not get any big ideas, Laura, because publishers pay a pittance to new writers and unless your book is a great success, you won't earn very much money from it.'

'Well, meanwhile she has to write it first,' I declared, giving Laura a friendly squeeze round her shoulders. 'But if she writes as well as she speaks, I'm sure her book will become a bestseller.'

All this talk had made me feel very randy and so without further ado I reached down and smoothed my hand over Bill's lithe, athletic frame and grabbed hold of his flaccid cock. I gently squeezed the velvet skinned shaft and straightaway his prick sprung up into a powerful erection. I clutched at his thick tadger and I swooped down to wash the uncapped helmet with my tongue.

He sighed ecstatically as I sucked greedily on his knob, dwelling on the ridge and sliding my tongue down the underside; I took his cock completely in my mouth in long, rolling sucks until I felt his shaft twitch wildly which signalled an oncoming spurt of spunk, so I opened my lips and lay back, pulling Bill's head down on to my bosom and he rolled his tongue around my nipples that were standing up like little red bullets and then he took hold of his purple-headed boner and eased the round knob between the pouting lips of my juicy pussey, propelling it in inch by inch until our pubic hairs were matted together.

With a deep cry he began to fuck me with powerful long lunges, spearing me deliciously

161

every time he slewed his shaft in and out of my squelchy slit. His thick truncheon stretched my cunney as we drove each other into a frenzy and he started to pump faster and faster as we rapidly approached the point of no return.

Suddenly his body stiffened and I clapped my hand over his firm, manly buttocks, keeping his cock deep inside my cunt, humping myself up and down as he exploded into me in a rush of liquid fire. With every throb of Bill's big cock, more and more spunk spurted against the walls of my love channel, mingling with my own love juices and my own climax came instantly as my swollen clitty sent ripples of bliss throughout my body and his still stiff prick finished me off in a series of delirious spends which made my cunt feel as if it were swirling and shuddering all round his jerking cock which continued to throb strongly inside my saturated sheath.

Who would have thought Bill would have so much spunk in him? I gently eased his prick out of my cunney and he replaced his tool with his tongue, flicking in and out of my honeypot which was overflowing with our love juices which were dripping down over my thighs. He brought me off again with his tongue and I returned the compliment, sucking him off and gulping down the sticky libation which came bubbling out of the tiny 'eye' of his massive knob. I smacked my lips and said to Laura, 'I do love the taste of spunk, it's the most invigorating of all tonics.'

And because I was concerned whether she knew how best to protect herself, I added, 'And of course, one never has to worry about any problems when fucking in this most delightful way.'

However, I did not need to worry about Laura for she caught the drift of my remark and said, 'Oh yes, Miss Jenny, but I so adore the feel of a hot, throbbing cock in my cunney, though I use linseed oil when necessary before I let a boy fuck me.'

[Linseed oil was a popular method of birth control in Edwardian times and is indeed an effective spermicide although the application could never be guaranteed and though Jenny Everleigh mentions her use of linseed oil in an earlier diary entry, she also favoured checking the monthly cycle and as far as possible abstained from the pleasures of the flesh during dangerous times. But what Edwardian girls would have given for an I.U.D. or the birth control pill – *Editor*]

We were now all ready to fall into the welcoming arms of Morpheus, but suddenly Kathie sat up sharply and exclaimed, 'My God! I've forgotten to say good-night to all the other guests! What will they think of me? I'd better put on some clothes and find out what's been going on!

'Hold on, my love, there's no need to worry,' said Bill sleepily, 'surely Marcella can do the honours for you.'

'But Laura said she was busy being fucked by Charlie, Gerry's black driver. No, I must see for myself that all is well,' insisted Kathie as she slid her legs over the side of the bed.

'Would you like me to come with you? It might

be less embarrassing if the two of us peek into the bedroom together,' I offered and Laura threw me a grateful look. 'Thank you, Jenny, that's a very kind thought, but it's hardly necessary and you must be very tired.'

'Oh I don't mind, and anyhow, we'll sleep late tomorrow,' I said as I heaved myself up out of bed, 'and we won't be missed here, Bill and Laura look out for the count.' And indeed, our fellow bedmates were already fast asleep by the time Kathie and I had put on our dressing gowns and tip-toed out back to Kathie's bedroom where Martin D'Elstree was slumbering peacefully.

We left him to his slumbers and opened the door of the first bedroom to find Tony Hammond and Gillian Glynne-Powell writhing together on the bed with the young archaeologist pumping his gleaming shaft doggie-style into Gillian's cunt from behind as she stood bending down with her outstretched hands flat on the side of the bed and her pert bum stuck up high in the air. The randy pair were so intent on their business that they did not even look up as we stepped back and closed the door upon the lusty couple.

Meanwhile in the second bedroom Geoffrey Manning was engaged in a luscious *soixante neuf* with Gerry Flynn who was lewdly sucking Geoffrey's mighty shaft whilst he was noisily slurping his tongue over her gorgeous love lips which were directly over his mouth.

'Well, the girls are obviously settled in for the night,' I said softly to Kathie as we withdrew from Geoffrey's room. 'Now this only leaves Marcella unaccounted for, and I think we know where she may be found.'

Kathie's lips creased into a wicked grin as she said, 'Marcella's in bed with Charlie, the naughty girl! I'd love to have a look at his big black cock, wouldn't you? However, I suppose that it would be rather unkind to interrupt them.'

The two of us looked at each other and then we burst out into an uncontrollable fit of giggles. 'Come on then, Jenny,' chuckled Kathie. 'I'm sure you want to see the sights as much as I do!'

So we padded across the landing to Marcella's room and very quietly opened the door and peeked our heads round to see an expected erotic exhibition – and we were not disappointed!

The lascivious girl was lying naked on the bed with Charlie, whose superbly muscular body was equally nude and she was frigging his swollen shaft with what appeared to be sperm-coated hands (Marcella later told us that Charlie had spunked three times before Kathie and I came in) and he was toying with Marcella's uptilted breasts which may not have been the largest the handsome West Indian had ever fondled but must have been amongst the most tempting with each jutting cone capped with a swollen dark red areola the size of a ripe strawberry.

Marcella released his magnificently thick cock from her grasp and turned over and lay on her belly, sticking her gorgeous backside high in the air. Charlie moved behind her and pulled her bum cheeks apart to lodge his huge black knob in the valley between them – and to my relief I saw that he did not try to go up her bum hole which surely would never have accommodated such a colossal cock without suffering some injury, but instead lodged his helmet firmly into her cunt, moving forward, back, then further forward into Marcella's voracious wet crack.

To her little cries of encouragement, he pushed and rammed home until the whole of his thick prick was enclosed in her cunt and then he let it rest still inside her clinging love channel, making his shaft throb in its tight receptacle until Marcella's cunney juiced up once more and she answered every forceful thrust of the delighted Barbadian with a wanton wriggle of her delightful bottom.

He clasped his arms around the delicious girl, taking a soft white breast in each hand, moulding them sensuously with his fingers and tweaking her upright titties to absolute perfection. Then his face contorted with the oncoming of his spend and with a guttural cry he ejaculated a flood of sperm inside her cunney and she heaved her bum up and down in rhythm to receive his copious emission with a most athletic abandon.

Kathie and I silently made our way out and closed the door behind us. 'All's well that ends well,' I said with a yawn. 'Now where shall we sleep? Would you like to go back and join Laura and Bill?'

'No, I don't think so. Let's go back and spend the rest of the night together in my bed,' said Kathie, a suggestion with which I was happy to comply. When we reached Kathie's bedroom we found that Martin had disappeared (we later found out that Mrs Hibbert had pulled him out of bed and at this very moment he was fucking the cook in the servants' quarters) and, with our nude bodies snuggled up to each other, we played with each other's titties and pussies for a while and the lines of John Donne, my favourite poet, came to mind, as I toyed with Kathie's large tawney nipples:

License my roving hands, and let them go
Behind, before, above, between, below.

Our mouths crushed together as I buried three fingers in Kathie's juicy cunney, rubbing her love lips with the other hand until they opened up fully and I was able to reach her swollen clitty which was standing up like a little pink soldier. She rocked her body backwards and forwards on my fingers and I thought to myself that I could probably insert my whole hand inside her dripping crack if I felt so inclined.

Her clitty was now incredibly hard and wet as I continued to tease it and keeping my fingers embedded inside her cunt, I could feel the vibrating heat and sticky goo of her honey as, thrusting, her hips upwards, she willed me to jab my fingers in and out of her sopping slit. Then suddenly Kathie arched her back and shuddered her way to a vigorous climax and though we both calmed down, we never stopped fondling each other's sticky, perspiring bodies until at last we fell asleep.

May 20th, 1909

None of the guests rose before nine o'clock this

167

morning though all the girls looked fresh and bright, unlike Tony, Bill, Geoffrey and Martin who in contrast were all bleary-faced and hollow-eyed. As aforesaid, whoever stated that the female is the weaker of the sexes is guilty of propagating an absurd fallacy!

We girls tucked into heaped plates of scrambled eggs, bacon, devilled kidneys and sausages from the row of silver dishes on the sideboard which were kept warm by tiny spirit lamps. But all the boys could manage was tea and buttered toast although Geoffrey Manning helped himself to some kedgeree [a breakfast dish that had been brought back from India consisting of cooked flaked fish, rice and hard-boiled eggs which was much favoured by upper-crust Edwardians – Editor].

'Anyone for tennis?' said Marcella brightly. 'Kathie and I have free use of our neighbour Major Sorrell's court whilst he is away in South Africa. The sun's shining and the exercise will do us good.'

I don't think the boys fully appreciated her suggestion but Martin had received a telegram informing him that some business in London required his urgent attention that afternoon so he excused himself and made his farewell. Bill and Tony gallantly agreed to play but Gillian and Gerry wanted to get back to Sidlesham and they too planned to leave the house.

Geoffrey Manning was more than happy to accompany me on a drive up to Cocking as I had a fancy to take a walk on the Downs, especially as this would allow him to drive the Rolls-Royce once more. As we were not needed to make up the numbers for tennis, this plan inconvenienced no one and of course Osbourne my driver was especially pleased because he would have yet more time to himself.

'I'll ask Laura if I can give her a hand,' he said as he held open the door of the car for me and I was tempted to say that I was sure he would give her more than a hand whilst the coast was clear! But I simply told him to be as helpful as possible and if that meant slewing his cock inside Laura's cunney, so be it, for I knew that Osbourne would never be guilty of the heinous sin of forcing his prick into a cunney which did not wish to receive it.

The dusty road was empty and Geoffrey drove at a fast lick, and at one time the speedometer touched seventy-five miles an hour! We parked the motor south of Cocking and tramped up to lonely Bepton. Geoffrey made pillows out of our rolled-up coats and seated on the heather, I gazed at the beauty all around us. The grass was purple with masses of imperial heath, thyme gave the air a grateful scent and small additions like the churr of a chaffinch and a Painted Lady majestically sailing by completed the wonderful picture.

Geoffrey was now dozing peacefully but I scrambled to my feet and walked up to the highest point where I could have a clear view for miles around us. The valley to the south was deep in the foliage of West Dean Woods and beyond them rose the great broad backs of the Downs. Under a near cloudless sky I peered across to the valley due south to see the spear-like spire of Chichester Cathedral. To the south west shone a silvery glimmer of sea and west and east were wooded heights.

I wandered down the other side of the hill and was startled to see the unusual sight of an artist, complete with paints, palette and easel, and his lady model who was posing by one of the saucer-shaped shallow pools of water known as dewponds which serve to water sheep and cattle.

You may ask, dear Diary, what was so unusual in an artist wishing to capture the beauty of a country lass against the exquisite background of the Downs. Well, whilst such a sight would not normally excite interest, this particular scene was different for not only was the pretty girl being captured on canvas stark naked but the handsome young artist was totally nude as well!

And what a good-looking couple they were – she was no more than twenty at most, as pretty as paint, with soft brown hair cascading down her shoulders framing her face, with lovely liquid chestnut eyes, a narrow, well-shaped nose and fine, regular teeth. She brushed the tresses of hair off her face and her superb young breasts, up-tilted with large tawny areolae and high-tipped erect nipples jounced up and down with the movement. At the base of her belly nestled a mass of auburn curls which frothed crisply around her pussey and her long legs were as sweetly shaped as any sculptor would wish to fashion.

The artist engaged on conveying the likeness of this paragon of female loveliness to canvas was perhaps a year or two her senior, slim, light-skinned and blue-eyed with a shock of blond hair, broad-chested and I also noted with appreciation the fine looking penis and heavy, hanging ballsack which dangled saucily between his legs. He turned round to dab some paint on his brush and this gave me a fair view of the firm, rounded cheeks of his buttocks.

I wanted to stay and watch this comely couple further, but it would have been quite inexcusable not to have made known my presence to them, so I called out, 'Hello there, would you mind if I watched you at work? I promise I won't interrupt.'

'This is public land, ma'am,' said the young man in a pleasant American drawl, 'and I guess you have equal right as Louise and myself to be here.'

They seemed totally unfazed by my presence and I thought it polite to introduce myself. 'Thank you, sir,' I said with an easy smile. 'My name is Jenny Everleigh. I don't think I have had the pleasure of making your acquaintance before now.'

'I'm Ashley Holmes of New York City, Miss Everleigh,' the handsome lad replied with a courteous little bow, 'and I have the honour to present a dear friend of mine, Miss Celia Harcourt-Sutfield of London.'

'We've met before,' said the gorgeous girl shyly. 'Count John Gewirtz kindly asked me to his fortieth birthday party last year.'

'Of course!' I said, going up to her and exchanging one of those rather silly feminine kisses with Celia, where one puckers the lips and kisses the air beside the other girl's ear. 'How very nice to see you again.'

Even though she was unclothed, I really should have remembered this delicious girl from Johnny Gewirtz's reception and dinner at the Ritz Hotel, for she was undoubtedly the prettiest of the clutch of girls at Johnny's table and I later saw her briefly during the wild late night gathering at the Count's luxurious house in Green Street, Mayfair. Although she looked demure enough, I recalled that Celia was by no means averse to sensual enjoyments and a small smile trembled over my lips as I remembered that at the Gewirtz celebrations, whilst I was on my back, enjoying the honour of being fucked by the Count himself, I noticed Celia on her knees gobbling the thick circumcised cock of Sir Ronnie Dunn whilst with her hands she was frigging the stiff, erect pricks of Lord Edward Aspith and Lieutenant Gerard Horne of the Household Cavalry.

'Ashley, why don't we take a short rest and offer Jenny some coffee from your thermos jug?' suggested Celia and though I hastened to say that I would not wish to disturb their work, the good-looking young Yankee insisted on my sitting down with them on the rugs they had placed over the grass, with their clothes neatly folded at the corners to prevent them blowing away, though this was hardly necessary as the warm early summer zephyr scarcely ruffled the lightest green stalks around us.

'I feel somewhat overdressed,' I said to Celia good-humouredly. 'I can understand why you are naked because you are posing for a picture, but I

172

must say I don't follow why Ashley has stripped off.'

'Oh, that's easily answered,' she said with a gay laugh. 'Just before you came over the brow of the hill, I asked Ashley to fuck me as I've had a great fancy for it ever since he picked me up from my Uncle George's nearby country house this morning. Uncle George is a good sport but my parents are also staying there so poor Ashley has been forced to take lodgings at a public house in Cocking.'

'It's been well worth it, darling,' said Ashley, sliding his arm round Celia's slim waist, 'and I can't wait to fuck your sweet little cunt again. Why it's been almost a month since we made love together in my apartment back in London.'

'Please don't let me stop you enjoying yourselves,' I said sincerely, 'after all, Celia has seen me being fucked by Count Gewirtz, though if you so prefer, I'll walk back over the hill where my friend is enjoying a quiet sleep.'

'No, no, Jenny, that isn't necessary, I assure you,' said Celia, whose eyes were now sparkling with unashamed sensuality. 'We don't mind an audience, do we, Ashley? Actually, I find the idea rather exciting!'

'Do carry on, then,' I smiled and sat back against the stump of a tree as the pair exchanged a burning kiss. Ashley's hands descended to Celia's pert breasts and rubbed his hand against her rising red nipples and she squeezed his rapidly rising shaft which fairly leaped into her grasp. She parted her thighs and I could see her superbly chiselled crack with its pouting pink lips peeking out from the curtain of silky brown hair. She squeaked with pleasure as he tenderly probed open the yielding flesh, sliding his fingers into her dainty cunt which was already moistening to accommodate them. She raised her buttocks slightly, showing herself wet and open, spread like a flower, inviting Ashley to fill her honeypot with his strong blue-veined cock. But Ashley was savouring the taste of her titties in his mouth and he continued to frig her with his fingers. Celia now bent her pretty head downwards to kiss the uncapped helmet of Ashley's shaft, which was of a sizeable thickness and though not the very biggest I have ever seen, was certainly of very acceptable proportions.

She sucked lustily on his large knob, her soft wet tongue rolling over and over the smooth rounded surface and I must admit that I was tempted to join in this libidinous game and my hands slowly travelled down my body to rub against my dampening pussey whilst I watched Celia suck half of Ashley's shaft between her lips as she fondled his hairy ballsack.

'Jenny, I know that Celia would love to have you play with her pussey and finish her off,' panted Ashley as he now straddled the lissome girl and I threw caution to the winds and ripped off my clothes until I was as naked as the lewd couple in front of me.

Then I wriggled along the grass until my face was inches away from Celia's exciting cunney which I now inspected at close quarters. Her splendid cunt was liberally covered with soft auburn hair but from the serrated red lips

174

projected quite three inches of stiff, fleshy clitty and I opened her love lips wider with my fingers and passed my tongue lasciviously around her very wet crack which made her body twist and buck like a caged beast.

'Oh God! I'm spending. I'm spending!' she wailed as she continued to gobble frantically on Ashley's twitching prick whilst I kept my tongue flicking inexorably against her salivating slit as I fingered my own wet honeypot and rubbed my clitty which had also swollen up nicely. Celia spent profusely all over my face whilst I tongued her clitty and brought her off in style and Ashley jetted his copious flow of creamy sperm into her mouth which she gulped down greedily, smacking her lips with glee as she tasted his salty masculine essence.

I achieved a smallish climax and the three of us were cooling down when a hoarse masculine cry floated down from the top of the hill. 'I say you three, what's going on down there?'

'Surely the man has eyes in his head,' chuckled Ashley as I told him that there was no need to worry because I recognised the voice as belonging to Geoffrey Manning who had obviously woken up and had gone searching for me.

Geoffrey walked briskly down the hill and when he reached us, he stopped and put his hands on his hips. 'What the deuce is happening here?' he repeated and I looked up at him with a roguish smile and answered, 'You can see for yourself, Geoffrey, I am engaging in a heavenly three-way fuck with Miss Celia Harcourt-Sutfield of London and Mr Ashley Holmes of New York.

Now I can only speak for myself, but if you so desire, I am almost certain that Celia and Ashley would be only too pleased to enlarge our trio into a quartet.'

'Yes indeeed, any friend of Jenny's is a friend of ours, Mr Manning,' said Ashley and Geoffrey's eyes gleamed as he said, 'Hold on a minute then, whilst I get undressed.'

Once he had stripped to the buff he sat down on the rug and Celia looked approvingly at the size of his fast-swelling shaft. 'Jenny, I do so love sucking off a nice juicy cock, would you mind if I gave these two fine pricks a good licking?'

'Please do so,' I said politely and with a grateful smile she grasped Geoffrey Manning's thick prick in her right hand and Ashley Holmes's lesser yet still sizeable weapon in her left and gave the two shafts a thorough frigging until they stood up like two throbbing flagpoles in her sticky grasp.

Then, getting down on her knees, she pulled the two cocks gently together and swallowed up both the gleaming uncapped helmets in her mouth, twirling her tongue over them both which caused the young men to sigh with pleasure. Their tadgers bounded and swelled in Celia's hands as she slicked her fists up and down their wet shafts and it was so stimulating to be sucked off in this way by this pretty minx that they spent almost simultaneously, spurting their fountains of hot, frothy jism into her willing mouth. She swallowed every last drop of their abundant emissions, milking their cocks until the two shafts had shrunk down to half-mast.

Celia snuggled down between them and I knelt

in front of the lovely girl to give her tingling cunney another good licking out. But Geoffrey gallantly volunteered to take my place, saying that he would be delighted to pay his respects to Celia's exquisite quim which pouted so provocatively from the silky brown bush which covered her mound so profusely.

However, within a minute or so, I noticed that Geoffrey's love truncheon had regained much of its stiffness as he happily slurped away on Celia's delicately sculpted pussey and so I slid on my back between his knees to frig his turgid tool. Ashley's cock had also now recovered much of its former strength and naturally he wished to partake of the goodies on display. So brandishing his stiffening shaft, he pulled himself across me to nudge the tip of his knob against the lips of my cunney. I swallowed the bulging red helmet of Geoffrey's cock between my lips so as to release my hands to guide Ashley's prick to its desired haven.

The double sensation of being fucked by Ashley whilst sucking off Geoffrey was most stimulating and my whole body tingled with erotic excitement as I went off into a crackling series of delightful spends. Ashley then began to shudder and his prick twitched irrepressively in my juicy sheath as we rocked together in a glorious mutual climax, made even more enjoyable moments later by Geoffrey who sent a stream of spunk gushing into my throat which I gulped down with gusto.

Celia now turned over on to her tummy and slipping some clothes underneath her, pushed out her delicious bum cheeks, parting her legs so we had fair view of her wrinkled little brown rear dimple winking away at us.

The boys slicked their hands up and down their flaccid pricks to stiffen them up for a further fuck, but only Geoffrey could manage to raise another hard-on. He positioned his throbbing shaft in the crevice between Celia's resplendent *rondeurs* and I took hold of his hot, smooth cock and washed my tongue over his knob before directing it towards Celia's bottom-hole. I stroked the pretty girl's elongated red nipples whilst alongside her Ashley dipped two long fingers between her pussey lips and began to finger-fuck the trembling girl.

Her hips jerked at the first nosing of Geoffrey's knob inside her bum-hole and she cried out, 'Ow! Ow! Your prick is too big, Geoffrey! Stop! Take it out! Aaah! No, no, you're in now, leave it in, that's lovely!'

His shaft was now firmly embedded in Celia's bottom, and from the exciting wrigglings of her rolling buttocks and from her flushed face and sparkling eyes, it was obvious that she was now thoroughly enjoying being corn-holed in this way, especially as I now sucked on her hard, erect titties and Ashley continued to diddle her juicy cunt.

Geoffrey's throbbing cock revelled in the tight-fitting fundament of this exquisite lass and he groaned, 'I'm in, oh, delicious! I'm landed and the spunk's coming up from my balls! Here it is – I can't stop!'

Knowing that his climax was near, Celia mashed her bum cheeks lasciviously against his belly as she called out, 'Oh yes, Geoffrey! Go on, spunk into my bum! Oooh, what a lovely warm fountain!' as he flooded her bum-hole with a fountain of creamy warm jism and brought her off to a magnificent orgasm.

We were now sated from our exertions and after refreshing ourselves with coffee from Ashley's thermos, we dressed ourselves and resolved to take lunch in Cocking. Ashley had a pony and trap stationed nearby and we arranged to meet again at Cocking Church which Ashley had discovered was noteworthy on account of an ancient mural painting that was well worth our attention. When Ashley and Celia arrived (naturally we were there first even though we had to walk back to the car) we trooped into the Church and examined the picture.

The painting is on a splay of a small Early Norman window and is intended to represent the appearance of the angel to the shepherds of Bethlehem. It shows two male figures, one tall and bearded, the other young, with both holding their crooks upside down. The older man is wearing a cloak and old-fashioned two-fingered gloves with which he shades his eyes as if dazzled by an apparition of which only two arms and the very tip of a large feathered wing remain, evidence enough however to say with a fair degree of certainty that they formed part of a drawing of an angel. And by the men's feet is painted a curious medieval dog sitting on its haunches and barking at the angel!

The surrounding scene has a wooden-looking line of conventional clouds, among which burns a cluster of flames. 'This fire was the thirteenth-century artist's conception of a star,' remarked Ashley as he pointed out a further feature of interest, a fine canopied wall-tomb also dating from the thirteenth century.

We left the church and decided to take luncheon at an inn just fifty yards or so down the road. We sat outside and ordered rounds of beef and cheese sandwiches and the men drank beer but Celia and I preferred tea which the landlord's wife offered to brew for us.

I went inside to use the inn's facilities and on my way back I noticed that the inn was as empty as when we had first come in, except for the one customer who we had passed by on our way out to the garden, a rather shabbily dressed young fellow eking out a half pint of beer and a hunk of dry bread for his midday meal, and I was curious to know what he was doing with the pile of leaflets which he had placed in front of him on the bar.

'May I have one of your pamphlets?' I asked him with a smile and he shrugged his shoulders and passed one to me, saying in a broad Sussex dialect which I will not attempt to reproduce in written form, 'If you like, Miss, but as you don't live round these parts, I don't think you'll find it very interesting as it's my election address. I'm standing for the parish council, you see.'

'Good for you,' I said, glancing quickly through the leaflet which was filled with fiery Socialist imprecations about the plight of the downtrodden peasantry. 'However, I wouldn't think you will gain much support round here with this sort of argument.'

He flashed an attractive grin at me and said, 'Don't frighten you, do I, Miss? I have to be very careful what I say because more than a few of the local farmers tell their people that I am a dangerous rabble-rouser and they've asked the magistrates to send me to prison for stirring up trouble, which they would too, if I gave them half a chance.'

'No, you don't frighten me,' I said patiently. 'My family has always been of a staunchly Liberal political persuasion, and I have genuine sympathy with the lot of the labouring classes. However, I must say that I understood that the condition of the country workers was slowly improving.'

The young man shook his head and was about to answer me when the landlord appeared and said, 'Now then, Eric Sargent, I've told you before I don't want no political talk in this bar, if you please, or I'll have to ban you like the other public houses in the village.'

'It's all right,' I said hastily to the landlord. 'It's not his fault because I began the conversation. Eric, my name is Jenny Everleigh. Come out in the garden and meet my friends. They'll be genuinely interested in your campaign. Would you like another glass of beer?'

He hesitated but I ordered the beer and when it was pulled from the pumps, I led Eric outside and introduced him to the others.

'My uncle, Mr George Harcourt-Sutfield, owns Muldoon House,' said Celia. 'I do hope he isn't one of your tyrannical employers who grind the faces of the poor into the dust.'

'No, that he's not,' admitted Eric with a broad smile. 'Mind, I couldn't say too much as my father's head coachman at Muldoon House and my mother often comes in to help with the cooking when Mr and Mrs Harcourt-Sutfield are giving a week-end party. We live in one of the cottages on the south side of the estate.'

'It must be a worry to your mother and father that Celia's uncle doesn't take umbrage at your political activities and put pressure on them to try and stop you campaigning,' remarked Geoffrey.

Eric sighed and said, 'That thought did cross my mind but to be fair, he hasn't even mentioned the matter to either of my parents, and truthfully, if all the other wealthy landowners were like Mr Harcourt-Sutfield, I wouldn't have a chance of getting in. He pays fair wages and keeps his labourers' cottages in good condition.'

And turning to Celia, he went on, 'If you want to see how badly some others treat their workers, you should look at the miserable condition of Sir Brindsley Hackshaw's dilapidated cottages. In bad weather, they get so damp that water trickles down the walls but none of the tenants dare to complain in case they get dismissed.

'How terrible,' said Ashley, offering Eric a beef sandwich. 'That mean-heartedness reminds me of our own American robber barons who stopped at nothing to squeeze a few bucks out of anyone who had the misfortune to be employed by them.'

Eric gratefully accepted the sandwich and said, 'Well, I'm lucky in that I have employment as a schoolmaster in Midhurst and I can't be forced out of my job by the likes of Sir Brindsley. Mind, if he makes any further threats against me or anyone who supports me, he'll find out that two can play at that game.'

This sounded intriguing and I asked Eric to explain himself. 'Well, on condition that you promise to keep what I tell you to yourselves, and as you're strangers in these parts, I don't mind saying that I caught Sir Brindsley in a very compromising situation with my Brownie.'

'Your Brownie?' asked a puzzled Ashley Holmes and I explained that this was the name given to the popular cheap Kodak camera. 'Go on, Eric, this sounds like a good story,' I said, resting my elbows on the table and cupping my cheeks in my hands.

'It is, Miss Everleigh, but how shall I tell the story to you?' he queried. 'If I repeat a certain conversation with total accuracy, there may be some words which offend.'

'Have no fear of offending us, Eric,' I said sweetly. 'In our circle we call a spade a spade.'

'Or even a fucking shovel!' added Geoffrey rather unnecessarily, though this did break the ice and proved again to me that a touch of indecency makes the whole world grin.

Eric sat down and took up his tale. 'It all began three weeks ago on a Sunday afternoon,' he said quietly as we gathered round to listen. 'I'd been tramping in Duncton Wood with my camera as I happen to be a keen photographer and I was looking for some suitable locations to photograph for a competition in the *Mid Sussex Gazette*.

'It was a warm, almost windless day and I thought I was the only person within a square mile when I heard a familiar voice coming from my right though I could not quite catch the words. So I moved towards the sounds and when I reached the edge of the small clearing from which the conversation had floated, I recognised the fruity tones of Sir Brindsley Hackshaw interspersed with a lighter-toned, feminine voice. I peered through the trees and saw Sir Brindsley sitting on a folding chair holding a sheaf of photographs. His trousers were down at his ankles and in front of him, frigging his bare shaft was a pretty young girl who I knew worked as a parlourmaid at his house.

'She was also half undressed, wearing only a white chemise with her coat, blouse and skirt folded neatly on a second chair. "Here, Penny," Sir Brindsley leered. "What do you think of these wonderful photographs which I bought from Hotten's last week? [Hotten's little bookshop in Piccadilly (not to be confused with Hatchard's) specialised in gallant literature for a coterie of wealthy trusted customers – *Editor*]

' "Look at this frisky French girl sitting stark naked on a chaise longue, pushing her rounded buttocks out towards the camera. Look at her, the cheeky cat, it's perfectly obvious that she's saying she wants a big stiff cock pushed in between those chubby bum cheeks and dammit, I'd pay good money to be the one to give it to her!'

' "That's nice," sniffed Penny, with a haughty flounce. "Here I am in the flesh, tossing you off and yet you seem to be more excited by a rotten old photograph. Don't I have just as pretty a backside as that French tart?" And to put Sir

184

Brindsley on the spot, Penny let go his prick and turned herself around, pulling up her chemise to show that she wasn't wearing any knickers and displaying the luscious cheeks of her nicely rounded arse to the randy old goat.

'She then turned back and undressed completely, pulling her chemise over her shoulders and, standing as she was just a few yards away from me, I must admit that her ripe young body certainly held my interest and I would have paid good money to be in Sir Brindsley's place!

' "Oh, your bottom's much nicer," said Sir Brindsley, "and so are all your other goodies. Let me take a good look at you, m'dear. Yes, you'd make a perfect model for any photographer with your wonderful big titties and that lovely little cunt nestling between your thighs.

' "But it's all covered up by that thick black bush of pussey hair. Let me brush it aside – ah, that's much better, now I can see those pouting cunney lips, all nice and juicy. I must salute them in the manner they deserve."

'With those words he stood up and then dropped to his knees, pushing her legs apart and nuzzling his head between her thighs. "M'mm, what a pungent feminine aroma," I heard him add as he kissed her hairy mound. "I'm going to bring you off, Penny, in just the way you like."

I moved round for a better view as he kissed her moistening cunney with his tongue running the full length of the parted love lips and Penny shuddered as he found her hardened clitty which stuck out like a miniature cock and I could hear him sucking and chewing it as she gasped for joy, her body jerking to and fro as she moaned, "Ooooh, Ooooh, Ooooh! More, sir, more please, I'm almost there!"

His hands gripped her hips as she twisted and writhed around, which must have made it too difficult for him to keep his mouth on her clitty so he moved his head from between her thighs and began rubbing and pinching her erect little love button with his thumb and forefinger.

' "Rub harder!" Penny cried out as her hands flew to her gorgeous naked breasts to play with her titties, massaging the elongated red nipples – and at this stage I took my first photograph of the randy Sir Brindsley with his chambermaid. My hands were trembling as I looked through the viewfinder but I managed to take three good shots as Penny's vibrations increased and she heaved and humped away until with an ear-piercing shriek she spent and she clasped her trembling thighs round Sir Brindsley's hands whilst the force of the spend coursed through her lovely body.

'But Penny's blood was up and she panted, "Now I'm good and ready to be fucked!" and she pulled him down to the soft earth and ran her nails along the length of his inner thighs and across his portly stomach. She moved close enough for her hardened nipples to graze his chest and then slowly moved down and, as his cock sprang up to greet her, she flicked at his knob with the tip of her tongue before twirling her tongue across his helmet.

'I took a further two photographs just as she started to suck lustily on Sir Brindsley's throbbing pole and he began jerking his hips up and down to thrust as much of his stiffstander as possible between her willing wet lips. Penny did a fine job for she managed to take in the whole of his thick prick right down to the root without gagging until his hairy balls dangled in front of her straining lips. Sir Brindsley grunted and groaned as he shot his load into Penny's mouth and she swallowed his creamy emissions with relish, and she gulped down all his tangy seed until his cock, milked dry by her exquisite sucking, began to lose its stiffness.

'The old bugger had the grace to thank her for his sucking off but she waved away his praise and said, "Oh, I enjoyed it – I love sucking cocks! I adore kissing the knob and sucking out the jism. I like the taste too and when the spunk squirts out, it's so exciting when it shoots into my mouth! I can't think of anything that tastes so fine and clean. The only problem is that none of you men can hold back for more than a few minutes." '

'I would have imagined that you would have given Penny anything she wanted if she would have sucked your own stiff prick,' commented Ashley a trifle cruelly.

'Absolutely so,' agreed Eric, 'but this thought flew only fleetingly across my mind. For I am engaged to Sally Reynolds whose parents keep a public house in Midhurst and it would not be right to play such games, however jolly, with any other girl.'

I was pleased to hear such words for as you know, diary, I eschew all extramarital activity and have never fucked with any engaged or married man with the sole exception of His Majesty King Edward VII, God Bless Him!

'Well, we might not be able to vote for you,' I said, opening my purse, 'but please do not take it amiss if we make a little contribution to the costs of your campaign.'

The others chorused their agreement and all expressed their willingness to contribute to such a cause and despite Eric Sargent's protests, I handed him five pounds which in the end he accepted with grateful thanks.

'I'll spend most of this on medicine to help the many people who suffer with rheumatism,' he said, expounding further on this subject when Geoffrey asked him if this was an illness endemic to the area. 'It certainly is,' Eric roundly declared. 'When not due to damp cottages it can generally be traced to exposure. The shepherd on the hills and the labourer on the farm frequently get soaked through in heavy rain, and not having the means of changing ready to hand, they continue to wear their clothes till they become dry again.

'You'll see a lot of old folk whose hands have been gnarled and whose bodies have been almost doubled up with rheumatism because they were compelled for the sake of their livelihood to wear wet clothes all day.'

'How awful,' said the horrified Celia and asked if there was any medical help afforded but Eric correctly informed her that there was no cure for rheumatism. 'However, a small bottle of spirits cheers the sufferer up no end,' said Eric. 'It helps dull the pain if nothing else.'

On that rather melancholic note, Geoffrey and

Ashley settled the bill between them and we said good-bye to Eric, whose chances of securing a few extra votes would surely be made brighter with the judicious distribution of a dozen or so bottles of whisky! However, just before we left the young modern-day Hampden, I asked Eric what he planned to do with the saucy photographs of Sir Brindsley and Penny the parlourmaid.

'Do you know, I'm not too sure about that,' he confessed. 'I'd far prefer to do nothing except keep them in my snapshot album, because I don't see myself as a blackmailer. But if Sir Brindsley Hackshaw starts putting any unfair pressure on my supporters, then I suppose I'll have to confront him with a set of prints and demand that he abides by the true spirit of the democratic process.'

Geoffrey clicked his fingers together and said, 'I've just thought of a good wheeze. Whilst you were telling us your story I suddenly remembered that I've met Sir Brindsley Hackshaw at the West Surrey cricket club functions. He used to be a keen cricketer in his younger days and he still turns out now and then for our second eleven.

'Now I've found that by and large, no chap who loves cricket can be a complete cad. So why don't Jenny and I visit Sir Brindsley and see if we can make him play the game fair and square as far as Eric is concerned? I'm sure he'll remember me from the last club dinner before Christmas which was a pretty wild affair. Come to think of it, he was sitting on the next table to mine.'

'Do you think he'll receive us?' I said doubtfully but Geoffrey gave a little chortle and replied, 'Oh yes, he'll be at home to anyone who attended that dinner, mark my words. If you haven't any other arrangements for this afternoon, Jenny, we might as well see if he's at home right now. Eric, how do I get to Sir Brindsley's place?'

'No, I've nothing planned and, as you say, there's no time like the present,' I said as I gave Eric my card and asked him to write to me with news of his campaign and Geoffrey and I also made our farewells to Ashley and Celia. We exchanged addresses and Celia made us all promise faithfully that we would keep in touch with one other in London, and she would make a dinner party the following month because Ashley was going back to New York in early November.

Then I settled myself in the car and Eric gave Geoffrey directions to get to Sir Brindsley's estate which was only about three miles away. On the way I asked Geoffrey why he had chuckled so heartily when he mentioned the cricket club dinner and though a wide grin appeared on his face, he did not answer my question.

'Come on, Geoffrey,' I insisted, and as I slid my hand across and pressed it down on his prick, I jokingly added, 'I have a very tender part of your anatomy between my fingers and you'd better spill the beans, or I might take an unfair advantage of my position.'

He smiled broadly and pulled the car into a lay-by. 'That's sheer blackmail,' he protested as I clutched hold of his cock. 'Ow! All right, Jenny, I surrender! I suppose I should tell all, you naughty girl, especially as I know you enjoy hearing about a full-blooded fuck!'

I gave his cock a friendly squeeze before replying, 'Well, don't we all? However, I've always preferred playing the game than being a mere spectator, although hearing a good story well told is a pleasant enough amusement.'

And with those words, I settled down in my seat as Geoffrey cleared his throat and explained what had taken place at this sporting function which was held at the village hall in Haslemere. It appeared that all went well until the tables were cleared, the speeches had been made, the annual presentations had been awarded and the port and brandy circulated freely amongst the seventy or so gentlemen there.

'Mr Reynolds, the club president, was in the chair and there was a great cheer when he stood up to speak because he was a very popular chap who always provided some *recherché* entertainment for the latter part of the evening.'

I interrupted him here and said, 'Mr Reynolds, did you say? Not Mr Michael Reynolds of the Holborn Business Machine Company by any chance?'

'Yes, that's the man, Jenny. Are you acquainted with him by any chance?'

'Sir Ronnie Dunn introduced Mr Reynolds to me at the Jim Jam Club a couple of years back during a Victor Pudendum competition,' I explained. [Readers of previous Jenny Everleigh memoirs will need no introduction to the Jim Jam Club, a semi-secret 'dining club' in Great Windmill Street, Soho, which boasted several highly placed pillars of London Society amongst its membership. Many wild parties were held there and in his younger days as Prince of Wales, King Edward VII visited the Club for the monthly 'Victor Pudendum' live sex show which is alluded to here – *Editor*]

Geoffrey looked at me with some surprise and said, 'Gosh, don't tell me that Mike actually took part in the show. He's a great cocksman but I would have thought he was too shy to display his prowess in public.'

'Oh no, Mr Reynolds did not take part in the actual competition, but he was sitting at our table with my dear friend Sally Randall whose verses appear occasionally in the *Tatler*. He was very much taken by the sight of Lady Charlotte MacGillergy bouncing up and down on Lord Finchley's prick whilst at the same time sucking Sir Knyston Didsbury's shaft and simultaneously frigging the cocks of Colonel Cavendish and Mr George Postlethwaite with her hands – so much so, in fact, that during the interval he whispered something in Sally's ear and minutes later when I left the table to go to the ladies' room, they also excused themselves and the last I saw of the pair that evening was seeing them charge upstairs to one of the *salle privées* for a good night's fucking.'

'That sounds like Mike Reynolds, he's always game for a bedroom frolic at any time, day or night,' grunted Geoffrey who then went on to describe what happened next at the cricket club dinner. 'Mike called for silence and whilst he was speaking, two waiters brought in a large mattress covered with a white sheet and placed it on the floor in front of the top table. Then he announced, ''Distinguished guests, gentlemen, may I have your attention, please. It is time now for our traditional after-dinner entertainment and it gives me especial pleasure to introduce the artistes who will perform for your delectation this evening for I know that you will all enjoy their performance. Gentlemen, please welcome Miss Gabby de Berri and Miss Alexa Bellini of Paris who will dance for us Monsieur Pierre Yougerputz's daring new work, *Le Ballet de Tribades*."

'He led what was frankly only a light smattering of applause because frankly, very few members of the audience were patrons of Covent Garden or Sadler's Wells. However, then Mr Grant's string quintet struck up a gay melody and two extremely pretty girls came dancing in dressed only in skimpy white coloured tops held up by thin shoulder straps and very short tutus so that the audience could see their legs, which were encased in white tights, way above their knees.

'Gabby was a striking girl, petite but with a pretty face framed by locks of auburn hair which tumbled over her cheeks whilst Alexa was taller with a willowy figure and was equally attractive with pert features and pouting rich lips, and those members of the audience at the rear of the hall stood up from their chairs to admire the graceful exhibition of the nubile girls' terpsichorean skills.

'At first there was a buzz of conversation from the audience but after what I can only describe as a collective intake of breath from the seventy-odd spectators, there followed a complete and absolute silence in the hall which was broken only by the soft, romantic music now being played by the small orchestra. For the two ballerinas had leaped upon the mattress and were now entwined in a passionate embrace on it, kissing and cuddling each other lasciviously as they slowly undressed themselves, sliding down their shoulder straps, peeling off their tights and unhooking their tutus until they were both nude save for their brief frilly knickers.

'I watched with great interest as Gabby tweaked up Alexa's big nipples to a fine erection as the taller, strawberry blonde girl slid her hands round Gabby's waist to grasp her deliciously rounded bum cheeks which she fondled with obvious delight. Alexa thrust up her titties in front of Gabby's lips and the petite, curvy minx licked and lapped on the elongated red cherries as Alexa now opened her legs to receive Gabby's hand on her neatly trimmed, light-coloured pubic bush.

'Gabby put her hands on the trembling girl's inner thighs and pulled them apart, displaying to perfection the pink outer lips of Alexa's cunt peaking through the silky moss which adorned her delicate notch. Alexa whimpered with pleasure as Gabby slid two long fingers into her juicy honeypot as she athletically leaped on top of her partner and straddled her so that the luscious cheeks of her backside were directly over Alexa's mouth. Gabby gently lowered her quivering bottom so that Alexa could take hold of her fleshy white buttocks in her hands and gently part them, allowing her to insert her tongue in the soft folds of her pussey.

'Now Gabby leaned forward and dived into Alexa's hairy muff, sucking furiously on her squelchy cunney to complete a perfect *soixante neuf*. The girls licked and lapped each other's cunnies, probing, sucking and frigging each other's clitties with their tongues, and they yelped with pleasure as they shuddered to a marvellous mutual climax.

'We all applauded this wonderful show as the girls continued to play with each other, grinding their pussies together and then Alexa climbed on top of Gabby who lay on her belly and rubbed herself on her gorgeous back and Alexa raised the cheeks of her own beautiful dimpled bottom to the assembled company and she opened her legs as she brought herself off so that her prominent sopping crack could be well seen by one and all.'

He paused and took a deep breath as I said with some slight irritability, 'Well, go on, Geoffrey, what happened next? I know how all you men dream of being the meat in a tribadic sandwich. Did Mr Reynolds shuck off his clothes and enter the fray?'

'Not exactly,' he said slowly and when I saw his cheeks colour up I guessed correctly what the dear boy was rather embarrassed to say!

'No, not exactly,' repeated Geoffrey, stroking his chin with his hand. 'As I think I said before, Mike Reynolds is rather shy and he just watched from his seat on the top table.'

'But you decided to lend a hand – and later your cock!' I giggled and Geoffrey sighed with relief when he saw that I was not disposed to think badly of him for his actions that evening.

'I'm afraid you're quite right, Jenny,' he admitted with a small lop-sided smile. 'Egged on by my comrades, I swiftly shed my clothes and stood by the mattress, waiting for the girls to invite me to join them. It was young Alexa who reached out for my throbbing stiff prick which was raised up high against my belly, and I moved forward and sank to my knees on the mattress as she pulled my shaft downwards to her mouth. She licked around the knob and then lashed her tongue round my rampant rod, slowly encompassing every inch until her lips touched my crisp pubic thatch.

'Gabby now turned over and straddled me so that her sopping wet pussey was directly over my lips, beckoning me irresistibly. I had only to raise my head an inch to work my mouth round her beautiful pouting slit and I inhaled with relish the musky feminine scent from her cunt as I lapped all round the edges of her dripping crack, rubbing my mouth against her cunney lips which drove the delightful girl into a veritable frenzy. "Please frig me with your 'ands, monsieur," she begged me in a sweet French accent and naturally I obliged, slipping three fingers into her sopping snatch.

'Meanwhile, to the cheers of the onlookers, Alexa was palating my prick with long rolling sucks and I could not hold back any longer and spent copiously, shooting an ample flood of frothy warm jism into her willing mouth. She gulped down my copious emission and turned away to frig the gnarled stiffstander of Jonathan Crawford, the club secretary, who had also thrown discretion and his clothing to the wind.

'However, I was still engaged in bringing off the lovely Gabby and I worked up a good rhythm as I finger-fucked her, slowly at first and then gradually increasing the pace as she slipped her own hand down to frig her clitty, rubbing the tiny rosebud between her thumb and forefinger. I replaced her fingers with my own as I now brought my other hand round to take over this clitoral stimulation whilst continuing to dip my fingers in and out of her juicy cunt whilst I also continued to lick and lap all around the red-lipped gash.

'Gabby let out yelps of pleasure as she reached her orgasm and her love juices flowed into my mouth and I lapped up her tangy spent until she was finally sated.'

Hearing about this sensual romp so fired my imagination that I suddenly realised that my knickers were now terribly damp and that I would have to take them off before we proceeded to go on to the Hackshaw's establishment. I lifted up my dress and managed to wriggle the wet garment down to my knees, at which point Geoffrey completed the job, pulling them over my feet and slinging them on the back window ledge.

'Don't let me leave them there, Geoffrey,' I said, glancing backwards. 'I wouldn't want Osbourne to see them lying there when he washes the car this evening.'

But my erstwhile storyteller was now also feeling decidedly randy and he tore open his fly buttons to bring out his throbbing great cock which shot out like a coil and I grasped the thick hard shaft with both my hands, rubbing the hot, smooth-skinned pole in my palms as Geoffrey embraced me and our tongues waggled madly inside each other's mouths. We broke off our kiss only to scramble between the seats into the back of the car where he rolled me over on to my back, threw up my skirt and chemise, and pulling down his trousers and pants, grabbed hold of his diamond hard shaft and rubbed his knob against my golden pussey hair.

I was really enjoying myself and my cunney lips were by now red and swollen with desire as with a deep groan he pistoned his magnificent sinewy cock straight into my welcoming cunt. His balls slapped against my bum as I wrapped my legs around his broad back and dug my nails in his shoulders.

We rolled around on the seat until I found myself on top and I placed my hands on Geoffrey's gleaming hairy chest as I rode him like a top jockey coaxing home a thoroughbred at nearby Goodwood racecourse. My cunney was now on fire as dear Geoffrey's big cock trembled and twitched in the manner which I knew heralded his spend. I felt his body go rigid and then he arched his back upwards and shot once, twice and then a third time as his spunk jetted out with such fierce intensity that I could imagine the sticky stream splashing off the rear wall of my love channel. Indeed, so abundant was his rivulet of jism that my thighs were well lathered as Geoffrey withdrew his shrinking shaft which rubbed itself amorously in a last salute against my pussey lips.

'Sorry about that, Jenny,' he muttered as he pulled up his pants and began to button up his trousers. 'I know you didn't spend but I just couldn't hold on any longer.'

'Don't worry,' I said in all truthfulness. 'I enjoyed the fuck immensely and it really didn't matter that I couldn't get there with you.'

Geoffrey still looked doubtful so I added, 'Oh, Geoffrey you silly boy, I'm not fibbing, honestly I'm not. Of course it's nice if we both climax, but spontaneous love-making like we just experienced is wonderful and it's simply an unfortunate fact of life that boys shoot up the ladder to a climax quicker than girls. Just because a girl doesn't have an orgasm, it doesn't mean to say she can't have a very pleasurable experience – which is exactly what I enjoyed just now.'

I think my words reassured him though all he said was, 'Well, I hope that's so, Jenny. Anyhow, we'd better dress ourselves before someone comes along and when we've finished we'll toddle down the road on our right which will take us to Hackshaw Hall.'

So we tidied ourselves up and as Geoffrey drove through down Hackshaw Hall's long, winding drive, I asked him if Sir Brindsley was a married man.

'Most certainly,' he replied, 'and frankly it is surprising that Sir Brindsley would have the strength let alone the desire to engage in extra-marital poking. His wife, Lady Sophia, is a beautiful Italian woman who he met whilst on a Grand Tour eight years ago. Their wedding was one of *the* London events of 1902. I'm surprised you don't remember it.'

'I was probably in Canada at the time,' I said. [*See* Jenny Everleigh 10: Canadian Capers – *Editor*]

'Well, Sophia is eleven years younger than Sir Brindsley and I have heard it said that she is a very passionate, hot-blooded lady, which you'd expect as she hails from Naples, though I should add that she is of noble birth, being a third cousin once removed of the King of Italy himself. She's a keen collector of Italian art and I understand she has several excellent paintings hanging in this house and in their London residence.'

I digested this information as we pulled up outside the front door of the splendid mansion. One of the house servants was passing by and Geoffrey called him over and asked him whether Sir Brindsley was at home.

'No sir, the master is in London until Thursday,' answered the footman. 'But Lady Sophia's here though I think she's busy in the greenhouse just now. But if you would like to give me your card, I will find her and see whether she wishes to see you.'

Geoffrey looked at me and I said quietly, 'Let's say hello to Lady Sophia whilst we're here. We can then judge if it's worthwhile mentioning the matter of Eric Sargent and ask her if she could persuade her husband to stop intimidating the voters – and I must say that I would feel far happier achieving our objective in this way than having to show Sir Brindsley the saucy photographs.'

He nodded his agreement and said to the footman, 'You don't have to bother about a card – my name is Charles Farnesbarnes of the Newman Gallery in Brighton and this lady is one of my senior colleagues. I am well-known to Lady

Sophia who is a regular patron of our establishment and indeed our business is rather with her than Sir Brindsley.'

The footman hesitated for a moment but his resistance collapsed when Geoffrey said with an irritable air of authority, 'Come, come, my good man. We've driven all across the county and we have a further appointment to keep before we motor back to Brighton this evening.'

So the footmen pointed the way to where Lady Sophia might be found and as we walked through the beautifully kept gardens, I asked Geoffrey why he had fibbed about our identity. He winked at me and explained, 'Well, firstly, I don't happen to have any visiting cards on me. Secondly, Lady Sophia doesn't know us from Adam and may not have wished to see us. And thirdly, whether or not she takes our side in this matter, the servants won't gossip about a strange couple turning up unannounced this afternoon, because I'm sure that Lady Sophia has her own artistic coterie.'

We followed the footman's directions and were walking through a narrow path through some dense shrubbery when I thought I heard a stifled groan from behind some nearby yellow bushes. I tugged at my companion's sleeve and whispered, 'Hold on a moment, Geoffrey! I thought I heard someone moan – there it is again, can you hear anything?'

He stood stock still for a moment, listened carefully, and then murmured softly, 'By Jove, you're right at that, my love. But the groans you hear are not coming from a damsel in distress – no, unless I'm much mistaken, these sounds are cries of fulfilment coming from a couple enjoying the fruits of sexual congress.'

As we moved quietly towards the source of the noise, I realised that Geoffrey was correct in his assessment of the source of the heavy breathing which was now clearly audible to us. Wouldn't it be extraordinary, I thought to myself, if we found Lady Sophia *in flagrante delicto* in the same way as Eric had discovered Sir Brindsley with Penny the parlourmaid.

The old saying about lightning not striking twice was disproved thirty seconds later when, from behind a bush, we pulled apart the dense foliage and lo and behold, what should we see but Lady Sophia herself on her knees with her mouth wide open as with her tongue she washed the thick, stiff shaft of a handsome youth who (and this judgement was soon to be confirmed) I assumed to be one of the under-gardeners, whose head was thrown back and who was gasping for joy as Lady Sophia bobbed her head to and fro as she sucked lustily on his glistening twitching tool.

They were both naked and I looked at the good-looking lad with a mixture of admiration and lust. He had been blessed with a pleasing, boyish face and a wide hairless chest together with slim flanks and shapely legs. And for one so young – I am sure he could not have been more than seventeen years of age – he boasted a very sizeable purple helmeted prick which rose majestically from the thatch of black hair at the root to stand almost straight up against his flat belly.

Lady Sophia may have been perhaps ten years

his senior but she was a fine figure of a woman. Her hair was very dark with a bluish tinge where it caught the light and the skin of her attractive face and gracefully curved body was smooth, of a delicate creamy tint which shone in the bright sunshine like polished ivory. And what gorgeous breasts she had, full and deep and tipped with big, erect bright red nipples each surrounded by rings of dark maroon-coloured areolae. I couldn't see her cunt which was hidden by a luxuriant fleece of long, soft brown pussey hair but my attention wandered back to her full red lips which had now ceased sucking the lad's throbbing boner but which were immediately replaced by her long, tapering fingers which smoothed their way slowly up and down his quivering cock. She said in a prettily accented voice, 'Ah, Thomas, your cock is truly *grandioso*! Such fine, smooth skin, yet so hard and stiff to the touch and quite large enough for a man of twice your age. Are you sure you've never used this *magnifico instrumento* for anything else except frigging?'

'No, my Lady,' replied young Thomas, his cheeks crimsoning as he went on, 'Hetty the dairymaid tossed me off last week after we had a kiss and cuddle, like, but that's as far as I've ever gone.'

'Then it is time you journeyed further down the path of love, Master Thomas,' breathed Lady Sophia as she made up an impoverished blanket on the grass by spreading out some of their clothes whilst she rolled up the rest to make one pillow upon which she laid her head and a second cushion which she placed under her buttocks.

With a wicked smile she beckoned Thomas to approach her and she parted her shapely legs and with her finger opened up the delectable red-lipped crack of her cunney for the lucky young lad. He knelt down in front of her and she gracefully lifted her foot to roll her toes around the mushroom helmet of his thick prick. Then she gently drew him over her and taking hold of his delicious cock, inserted his knob between her waiting cunney lips as the dimpled cheeks of his tight little bum fairly shook with anticipation.

How they sighed and moaned as they enjoyed this *al fresco* fuck! Although this was his first experience, like most country boys, Tommy had a natural understanding of what was expected of him and did not, like so many boys of his age, slide his cock in and out in a mad frenzy of lust, but thrust home at a slower pace which had the desired effect on Lady Sophia who was now in a high state of high excitement.

'Aaah! *Sfarzoso! Splendido!* Fuck me, Tommy! Empty your balls, big boy!' she screamed out, oblivious now as to who might hear her as her bottom rolled from side to side and she clawed the boy's back with her nails as he grasped her shoulders and rode her like a bucking bronco. Her legs slid down as she arched her back, working her seething slit back and forth against the pounding of Tommy's eager cock.

We watched with mounting interest sliding in and out of Lady Sophia's cunney and Geoffrey muttered sarcastically, 'What a shame we didn't bring a camera, Jenny. I'm sure the editor of the *Mid Sussex Gazette* would have been overjoyed to print a picture showing the mistress of the local squire and the gardener's boy hard at work in the garden, especially if we could persuade Eric to send him a snap showing Sir Brindsley similarly engaged in exercise with the parlourmaid!'

'It would send up his paper's circulation,' I giggled as we watched Lady Sophia caress Tommy's balls whilst she writhed and twisted in the throes of her climax as he continued to slam his tool in and out of her tingling pussey. The soft touch of her hand on his ballsack sent the spunk flying upwards through his shaft and with a hoarse little yelp he spurted spasm after spasm of spunk inside her sopping slit. His spend was so powerful that it appeared his slim body was being shaken to pieces as he thrust forward one more time and then collapsed in a state of total exhaustion on top of his mentor.

But Lady Sophia was keen to carry on and she rubbed the youth's limp prick in her hands until it again stood up hard and stiff and she said, 'You are a natural fucker, Tommy, I must congratulate you on your performance. I came twice before you spunked which is more than I can say as far as my husband is concerned. He squirts his juice whenever he pleases without any regard for my needs.

'So I would love to be fucked again, young man,' she added, squeezing his shaft sensuously as she laid back and guided his uncapped knob between the portals of the flushed, pouting lips of her ripe cunney.

Tommy was happy to oblige and he fucked her with renewed power, plunging his prick in and out of her sopping cunt, his balls banging against her bum as his shaft slid all the way in to the very root. She responded with equal vigour, meeting his thrusts with energetic heaves, and she urged him to thrust deeper as the bawdy pair revelled in their voluptuous delights. The willing lad pumped his raging tadger in great pistoning strokes until she clasped his shoulders and told him to slow down as she wished to change position. This puzzled Tommy but he kept his rigid cock sheathed inside her juicy cunney as she pulled him over and somehow keeping his shaft embedded in her cunt, she lifted herself on top of him, straddling herself across his thighs and squeezing her own thighs together to keep his twitching prick in place.

'Lady Sophia must be an expert horsewoman,' I said softly to Geoffrey, for the mistress of Hackshaw Hall was riding young Tommy's cock in great style, twisting her hips and bumping and grinding away, before leaning forward to offer him her erect nipples to suck which drove her completely wild when he began lapping at the succulent red cherries.

'Spunk into me, Tommy!' she cried out, rocking backwards and forward on his pulsing prick, thrashing about as if almost demented until they ran their delightful course through to the finish in a glorious mutual spend.

'Did you enjoy that, ma'am?' asked Tommy shyly, whose shrunken cock was still inside his lusty lady's tingling love channel. 'I didn't know that the man could lay on his back and let the girl do all the work.'

Lady Sophia laughed aloud and playfully pinched his cheeks. 'Ah, you English are so hypocritical!' she answered him gaily. 'All you young people are taught about fucking is the basic "missionary" position, as I think you call it, but wealthy boys are encouraged to learn all about the refinements of love-making from foreigners!

'Still, I am more than happy to be your instructress, Tommy. Sir Brindsley doesn't like me riding him – the silly man believes it is an affront to his masculine pride to let his wife assume the dominant position. But I have told him that dominance has nothing to do with it. I just love sitting down and working my cunney round a strong hard cock, because when I am grinding my bottom about, I am giving my clitty a good rub as well.'

Now I must blush, diary, for I did something very foolish though fortunately (as you will see) no harm came from my rash behaviour. For unable to contain myself, I showed my approval of this fine speech by clapping my hands and calling out, 'Hear, hear! Well said!'

This ill-timed intervention caused Lady Sophia to spring up from her seat on Thomas's thighs and snatching up her dress which she held in front of her to cover her nudity, she gasped, 'Who's there behind the bush? Come out and show yourself immediately!'

Shamefacedly, I stood up and walked towards her, followed by Geoffrey who cleared his throat and said, 'Good afternoon, Lady Sophia. I must apologise for the fact that my friend and I have been inadvertent spectators of, ah, your activities but we were about to withdraw when, um –'

'I simply could not stop myself applauding your sentiments, Lady Sophia,' I interrupted, offering my hand to the bewildered girl. 'And may I also congratulate you on initiating this luscious young man into the joys of *l'art de faire l'amour*. It looked so enjoyable that I wanted to tear off all my clothes and join in.'

These warm words mollified the Italian beauty and she relaxed visibly as I went on, 'May we introduce ourselves – this gentleman is Mr Geoffrey Manning and my name is Jenny Everleigh. We are staying in Westhampnett for a few days but Geoffrey and I decided to spend this lovely day on the Downs.'

Geoffrey had the good sense to retire whilst Lady Sophia began to dress herself and I continued to tell her of our meeting with a local man in Cocking which made us decide to see if we could speak with her – 'about a delicate matter,' I said, flashing a look to the still naked Tommy who was sitting up gawping at us.

Lady Sophia caught my drift and she told Tommy to dress himself and be off – and I noticed that she slipped a sovereign into the youth's hand as he left, a kind act which was surely a good omen for our mission as it showed her to be a woman of generous spirit.

'So what is your business with me?' she asked as Geoffrey rejoined us and we strode back briskly towards the house. 'I hope you are not going to ask me for favours to keep this afternoon's episode from my husband?'

'Certainly not, you may rest assured our lips are sealed,' said Geoffrey, which reassured her immensely. 'But it is about your husband that I have come to see you.'

'Let's talk about it over tea,' she suggested and I was glad to accept her invitation because watching all that splendid fucking had made my mouth and throat quite dry! She showed us in to the drawing room and after ordering tea, she settled down in her chair to listen to what we had to say.

Geoffrey explained the situation to her – though naturally he said nothing about Sir Brindsley's tryst with one of the parlourmaids at Hackshaw Hall – and it was soon obvious where Lady Sophia's sympathies lay.

'I would love to help you,' she said, spreading out her hands, 'but I regret that my husband is absurdly narrow minded about these matters. I have spoken to him before about the poor state of our farmworkers' homes but he says that the old world character of Downland cottages will be destroyed if he pulls them down and builds ugly modern brick dwellings in their place. He maintains that no one has complained to his steward and is convinced that the labourers on the estate are quite contented and have little desire above anything other than work, drink and their own rustic amusements and are perfectly contented to let their more favoured superiors govern the country and administer the law of the land.'

'If that is so, why is he so frightened that Mr Sargent might secure a seat on the parish council?' I demanded which made Lady Sophia throw her arms out in the air and say, 'I know, it makes no sense. If our workers were happy, they would not want to vote for the Socialists.

'Yet my husband is not an unkind man but he lacks the necessary imagination to throw off outdated beliefs which he has inherited from his family. But I promise you that I shall speak again to Brindsley and attempt to persuade him that he must ignore the cold dictates of his head and let the warm, loving instincts of his heart take precedence.

'And I think I know the best way to achieve this goal. Unless he makes instant repairs to the cottages, I shall refuse to suck his prick.'

Geoffrey blanched and said to her, 'Oh dear, Lady Sophia, I really don't want to be the cause of an argument between husband and wife.'

She told him that he should not worry about this and to our surprise she added, 'Brindsley doesn't deserve any treats in bed because I am certain that he has been fucking Penny, one of our parlourmaids. This is why I let myself be tempted by Tommy this afternoon. How do you say in English, what's sauce for the goose is sauce for the gander, yes?'

The subject of this conversation, Penny, and another maid brought in tea before either Geoffrey or I could reply and I changed the subject by admiring the pictures which adorned the walls of the beautifully appointed room. I particularly admired the portrait of an extremely good-looking girl in sixteenth-century dress and I wondered who had executed the painting.

'Was he one of the Dutch masters?' I asked but Lady Sophia shook her head and said, 'I'm pleased to tell you that the artist was neither Dutch nor male. We cannot be too sure but most experts who have seen the picture – which I bought quite cheaply in Italy – say it is by one of the Anguissola sisters from Cremona.'

This unusual foreign name rang a bell – where had I heard it before? And then I remembered that I had come across it in the saucy confession of Merida Hatfield in the *Cremorne* magazine I had read whilst my driver Osbourne had gone to fetch help after one of our back tyres had suffered a puncture on our journey down to Chichester.

I mentioned this fact to Lady Sophia who, to my surprise for I would not have thought she would have even known about such a saucy publication as the *Cremorne* said, 'Yes I read that letter from Merida Hatfield and invited her and her employer, the art critic, Sir Felton Renshaw, to come here and see the picture for themselves because opinion is still divided as to which of the sisters might have painted that picture.'

'Who were these sisters?' asked Geoffrey curiously as he scanned the colourful portrait. 'I've never heard of them, though there can be no doubt that whoever painted this picture was an artist of the first rank.'

'Oh, the Anguissola girls were all talented artists in sixteenth-century Italy,' explained Lady Sophia. 'There were six of them and they came from a poor but noble family, so they were encouraged to develop their talents in case their small dowries left them without husbands.

'The most famous of all was Sofonisba, in whom Sir Felton Renshaw and Merida Hatfield are especially interested. She was a child prodigy who was apprenticed for three years to the painter Campi and soon became famous in her own right. She taught her sisters how to paint and two of them, Lucia and Europa, became almost as famous and won many Church commissions. But when Sofonisba was twenty-six, she accepted an invitation from King Philip the Second of Spain to work for him in Madrid and she became very wealthy, painting him, his family and members of his court.

'She married a Sicilian nobleman and returned home but unfortunately most of her Spanish paintings have disappeared. She carried on painting till she was very old; when she was struck down with blindness; she retained a lively interest in art and many famous artists, including Van Dyck, who visited her home and wrote that he learned more about art from Sofonisba than from any of his teachers.'

I studied the portrait and said, 'Do you think this could be a self-portrait of Sofonisba or one of her sisters?'

'Quite possibly,' answered Lady Sophia, who was obviously a great fan of the Anguissola girls. 'Sofonisba certainly had a shrewd eye for publicity and sent the Pope a self-portrait as a gift which helped her sisters obtain work from the Church. But above all she had enormous talent. Giorgio Vasari, one of the most important critics of the age, once said that the figures in her paintings lacked only speech to be alive and I truly believe that she is one of the many women painters whose magnificent pictures have been quite deliberately ignored by blinkered male critics who wanted to minimise the contribution of women to art.'

'I do so agree with you,' said Geoffrey, picking up a copy of the *Nineteenth Century* from an exquisite mahogany occasional table. 'Even in such a distinguished magazine as this, which I happened to read last week we can find supposedly intelligent men writing against female emancipation and a universal suffrage in these words: "We must look facts in the face. However long it may take the woman of the future to recover the ground lost in the psychological race of the past, it must take many centuries for heredity to produce the missing five ounces of female brain."

'But in my humble opinion, the reactionaries are fighting a losing battle. Society is progressing so quickly that the rift between the sexes can only be eliminated if women are given the chance to compete on equal terms. Even some of the diehards now realise that the choice is not between going on and standing still, it is between advancing and retreating.'

And on this rousing note we took our leave, though Lady Sophia insisted on taking our addresses and said she would contact us when she next came up to London.

We drove back to Westhampnett and when Geoffrey pulled to a halt in front of our hostesses' motor-house, I remarked to him that I thought it was now time that the guests should soon make their way back to London. 'I wouldn't want to outstay our welcome,' I said as I stepped out of the car. 'Kathie and Marcella's hospitality is beyond question but I'm sure they would like to get back to their daily routine.'

'You could well be right there,' agreed Geoffrey as he gave me back the keys of the Rolls-Royce. 'I thought in any case, I had planned to leave tomorrow after luncheon as I have a shareholders' meeting to attend the next morning.'

Somehow I had assumed that Geoffrey had independent means though heaven knows, my family have never looked down upon those engaged in trade. 'Are you a company director?' I said with interest but he shook his head and smiled, saying, 'Oh no, nothing as grand as that. It's just that my grandfather left me a parcel of shares in Stoughton and Priestley Manufacturing in his will and I thought it might be interesting to hear what the firm is up to. I say, Jenny, if you're at all interested, do come along and we can have luncheon together afterwards.'

In fact, diary, that is exactly what I did do which is how Geoffrey and I came to be in bed together as described at the beginning of this chapter of my reminiscences.

However, before I lay down my pen, I must add a short coda about the final fling we enjoyed on this long, lazy weekend spent with my kind friends, Kathie and Marcella.

Before we dined I informed the girls that I would have to leave the next day. They tried to dissuade me and suggested I stayed on a few more days but I said that I had to return home to fulfil other social engagements. As it happens, Tony Hammond and Bill Massey had also said they were leaving tomorrow, which confirmed the correctness of my decision to leave.

After an excellent roast duck dinner, Tony stood up and holding a glass of wine in his hand, proposed the health of our kind hostesses, a toast which was drunk with many a 'hear, hear,' and 'they are jolly good fellows' from his fellow guests.

However, the handsome young archaeologist did not sit down but kept on his feet and knocked on the table for silence. His face was somewhat flushed for he had consumed the best part of a bottle of wine as well as two double whiskies before dinner, though he was in a merry mood rather than in a sozzled state, if I may be permitted to make this fine distinction.

Anyway, he called for silence and said a little indistinctly, 'Ladies and gentlemen, we've drunk to the health and wealth of Kathie and Marcella and that's only right and proper. But may I be permitted to say a few words of appreciation of Mrs Hibbert, whose culinary arts have been so enjoyed by all members of this distinguished company. The duck was delicious, was it not? Actually, that reminds me of an old poem:

There was a young lady of Glasgow,
Who fondly her lover did ask, Oh,
  Pray allow me a fuck,
  But she said, 'No, my duck,
Though you may, if you please, up my bum go!

215

'However, I digress, my dear friends. It is time now for the final course of this munificent repast and I have great pleasure in bringing in the dessert trolley myself.'

He marched a trifle unsteadily to the door and for a moment I wondered why on earth he should take it upon himself to do so. But in an instant I realised what Tony had in mind because Laura and the other servants had quietly retired and we would have to help ourselves to our puddings.

My speculation that Tony had conspired with Mrs Hibbert to provide a naughty *bombe surprise* was proved correct when he pushed in a large trolley covered by a table-cloth. With a suitable extravagant gesture he whipped off the cloth to reveal the gorgeous naked body of Laura the young housemaid, whose only attire consisted a judicious placing of strawberries smothered in cream which partially screened her own succulent nipples and a delicately positioned arrangement of blackberries and raspberries resting on her glossy russet-haired pubic mound, topped off by an impudent-looking banana which protruded so invitingly from her pussey lips.

We heartily applauded Tony's idea to finish our last meal together with a grand all-in fuck, and we insisted that he began the proceedings by consuming the banana which now wiggled lasciviously as Laura clenched and unclenched her thighs.

So to a fine rousing cheer, Tony slipped off his jacket and pulled the unprotesting Laura's legs round off the trolley before placing her ankles on his shoulders. Then he dived forward and holding the laughing girl round the waist, he gulped down the banana until he reached the crisp chestnut hairs of her delectable pussey.

He plunged his face into the arrangement of berries and began licking and lapping at her sweet smelling cunney lips. As he did so, Bill Massey joined in the fun by leaning forward and flicking off the strawberries from Laura's nipples and sucking noisily upon her engorged, stiff titties whilst Tony continued to nibble around the pouting lips of her cunt.

'Ooooh! How lewd!' gasped Laura as she trembled all over from this joint oral stimulation. I moved slightly to my right to see the tip of Tony's tongue parting her crimson cunney lips, seeking the moist cleft where I guessed her clitty was already bursting out of its shell. Her rounded bum cheeks squirmed deliciously on the table as Tony's tongue washed all round her swollen love bud and tiny rivulets of love juice soon started to trickle down Laura's inner thighs.

This erotic exhibition set us all off and when I glanced to my left I saw that Kathie and Marcella were vying for possession of Geoffrey's throbbing tool which he had released from the confines of his trousers. Kathie's lovely rich lips were spread around his naked uncapped knob whilst Marcella was jerking her closed fist up and down his thick smooth-skinned shaft. Their efforts were soon rewarded when Geoffrey spunked in short, sharp bursts which Kathie gulped down, continuing to suck on his pulsating prick until it finally began to go limp.

We finished with a glorious 'daisy chain' in

which Geoffrey fucked Kathie whilst she sucked Marcella's stiffly erect nipples. At the same time, Marcella's cunney was being lovingly filled from behind by Tony's majestic tool, with my head between his legs, sucking his heavy balls whilst Bill fucked me and frigged Laura's love channel as she played with my aroused titties.

In the end, after each and every one of us had given complete satisfaction to our partners, we collapsed in a sweaty, naked heap of bodies and as I wiped the perspiration off my brow I said to Bill Massey that perhaps we had overdone things a little after a heavy meal.

'I don't think so, dear Jenny,' he gently replied. *'Quando viene il desiderio, non è mai troppo!'**

TO BE CONTINUED

* When desire comes, it is never excessive.

218